# DAWNSPELL

## BRIDGE OF LEGENDS

### BOOK TWO

## SARAH K. L. WILSON

This is a work of fiction. All characters, places, and events are purely fictitious.

**DAWNSPELL**

**Copyright 2019 Sarah K. L. Wilson**

ISBN: 978-0-9878502-8-7

Cover art by POLAR ENGINE

Map by Francesca Baerald

Appendix art by Harold Trammel

**www.sarahklwilson.com**

Direct comments or feedback to
sarah@sarahklwilson.com.

For Cale

Always

# LEGENDS

### BYRON BRONZEBOW
*A good-looking hero who carries a bronze bow. Known in history for his care for the poor and needy.*

### DEATHLESS PIRATE
*Known for his love of treasure and invulnerability and recognized by his hook for a hand and belt of human skulls.*

### GRANDFATHER TIMELESS
*Based in the Timekeepers religion he is known for his high hat, long black coat and golden waistcoat. He is Time in human form subjecting all to his will.*

### KING ABELMEYER THE ONE-EYED
*Known for his single eye and broken crown, King Abelmeyer united the five cities of the Dragonblood Plains in the alliance that lasts today.*

### LADY SACRIFICE
*Known for her loveliness, innocence and sacrifice for the people, she is usually clad in a white dress.*

### LILA CHERRYLOCKS

*A master thief and trickster. Known for her long cherry-red locks, deft skills, and adventurous spirit.*

### MAID CHAOS

*The right hand of Death. Known for destruction, death and the golden breastplate she wears.*

### QUEEN MER

*Queen of the Sea and mother to the Waverunners. Queen Mer is known for her revenge upon man in the form of hurricanes and typhoons and for the shells, scales, and seaweed that she wears.*

### RAM THE HUNTER

*The unspoken Legend. Not mentioned in the Dragonblood Plains except in whispers, he is known for slaying dragons and going insane in the aftermath.*

# 1: ADRIFT

## *MARIELLE*

Marielle flinched before thinking – before realizing the shadow she saw was nothing more than a swooping gull. Not the dragon. Nothing more than a carrion-eater.

Marielle's head spun under the hot sun. It wasn't the heat so much as it was the smell. Two days after the dragon Jingen had risen into the air and destroyed Jingen City, and the dead were still bobbing up to the surface of the sea. Two days and the brackish water still stank of chaos and fear, rising in horrible puffs of red and black scent that filled Marielle's nose with vinegar and smoke. She coughed – again – adjusting the scarf Jhinn had given her and breaking her rhythm with the oars. The scarf wrapped around her nose and mouth wasn't enough to break the scent – not even to mask it.

"You got to keep your oar in the water or we're never gonna get free of this mess," Jhinn said from the back of the gondola.

But he was on edge, too. They weren't the only boat to have narrowly missed the dragon's flaming rage that first night.

They'd barely managed to beat the flames from the gondola. Luckily, they hadn't been the target. It had been another raft of people fleeing the chaos of Jingen that the dragon had targeted, another raft of desperate survivors who had gone up like a lit torch in the water.

The gondola swayed in the high, frothy waves as water broke over its low bow. And Marielle flinched, the memories still too strong not to make her shy away from the smallest violence. The gondola wasn't made for big water.

"If we row far enough, a current will catch us and we can drift south of the cities." Jhinn had been saying that every hour for a day.

Marielle pulled harder on her oars. Anything to avoid thinking about returning to the five cities. She couldn't face them. Every bloated body that drifted by was her fault. The clouds of squawking gulls fighting bitter battles over the remains of the dead were because of her. If she had only died back there, everyone else would have lived. If she had only died back there, they wouldn't be fleeing a raging dragon, an easy target for him as they bobbed on the rough sea.

If Tamerlan hadn't saved her life…

Not that she'd had much choice when he threw her over his shoulder and fought his way to the top of the Palace.

Her gaze drifted to where he lay on the floor of the boat, sea spray soaking him, muttering under his breath as the sweat of a fever beaded across his pale forehead.

"Dragon," he muttered, barely audible over the crashing waves as the little boat swelled up on the top of one only to come crashing down on the other side, jostling them all and clattering Marielle's teeth together, intensifying her headache. "Must kill the dragon."

If only he'd killed the dragon back at the Seven Suns Palace. If only he'd done that instead of setting her free. Then maybe all these people wouldn't have died.

She'd stopped looking at individual bodies. She couldn't bear it after the first few. She could feel madness calling to her through the guilt and despair she felt at the sight of them. And she was worried that if she looked – if she saw one more face that was almost familiar, if she saw one more little body too small to be an adult's – she might not keep her mind long enough to help Jhinn and Tamerlan to safety. She owed them that much at least. After all, they'd been trying to help her. They hadn't known what that would mean for the rest of the city.

And to save them, she might have to return to the cities, despite what Jhinn thought. Despite her bone-deep shame. Tamerlan was looking worse by the hour and heading into the waves was long, slow work.

Tamerlan hadn't known he would be freeing a dragon, letting him loose to blaze his wrath in the night on the unsuspecting. To be fair, neither had she.

"Where do you think the dragon is," she said again. She said it almost every hour since he disappeared a day ago. She said it

3

so much that she thought she was saying it even when she was silent.

"Not here. That's all that matters," Jhinn said. "I thought that perhaps he was heading to the mountains."

What would a dragon want with mountains? There was nothing there. Nothing but cold and silence. Maybe that was what he wanted. Marielle was pretty sure there were still buildings stuck to his back like barnacles when last they'd seen him setting ships on fire.

She swallowed as their little boat hit another swell, lifting up in the waves, broken wood and tangled debris lifting up with them. From this height, she could see the distant white sails. A fleet had arrived the same night that their city had been destroyed. A fleet of mysterious ships that remained out in the distance two days after their arrival. The sight of them formed a knot in her belly. Merchants wouldn't sail in such numbers or wait so far out. What could they want from the five cities?

She'd seen a ship leaving Jingen at dawn on the first day and Jhinn had thought that perhaps that ship was going out to greet the fleet, but it had headed north instead, toward Xin. She'd wondered if it was full of refugees until Jhinn pointed out the Lord Mythos' banner on the flag. A ship of Landholds or government officials was much more likely than refugees. And they'd carved through the survivors in the water like they were driftwood, never pausing for a moment to haul anyone else aboard. That had made her stomach turn. The wealthy always got what they needed at the expense of the rest – even now when they were all ruined, rich and poor alike.

Despite Jhinn's insistence that they could go south if they got far enough out, the current was dragging them ever north and east, out past the Jingen cliffs to where she could almost make out the arm of the Cerulean River flowing into the ocean in the Bay of Tears.

Every other boat she'd seen – and there weren't nearly as many as she'd hoped there would be – had been making toward the Bay of Tears just like that government ship. By that route, Xin City wasn't far. Help would be in Xin – or at least commerce – and right now Marielle thought that would be a good thing. Tamerlan needed help from a real healer.

She swallowed, looking down at Tamerlan as she rowed. How long would he last with a fever like that? She'd tried to poultice his wound and keep it clean, but in the bottom of the boat, constantly sprayed by ocean water – ocean water that was filled with the dead – it was easy to see how infection had set in.

"We should turn to Xin," she said for the third time that hour, shuddering at the thought even as she spoke the words. "I think Tamerlan needs a healer."

"It will be impossible to find one in the surge of refugees. We can tend to him here. He can fight this off." That was what Jhinn had said in response every time. He sounded as tired by it as Marielle was.

Their boat crashed down the wave, and Marielle's belly turned with the spin of the little craft as Jhinn steered them into another set of breakers. She glanced back at his stony expression. He wasn't going to change his mind on trying to flee the five cities. A boy with a look on his face like that one had made up his mind. Even with the waves and current fighting them constantly for the past two days, Jhinn remained set on the course.

"I'm not sure he has the strength to fight it." Her belly knotted at the thought. She'd changed his dressing twice today and it was still spotted with blood and yellow puss. That couldn't be good.

"Why did he fight like he did when he rescued me? So strong and mighty one minute, and then weak the next?" she asked Jhinn.

"All I know is that he saved me when no one else cared. They were going to sink my gondola – two Watch Officers," Jhinn explained as they rowed. "You know I can't go ashore. And there were no other boats near who could take me. Maybe one would have happened by while I swam. Maybe not. It might have killed me."

"He killed a lot of people in the Temple District," Marielle said, still not able to balance Tamerlan the kind-hearted savior of both her and Jhinn with Tamerlan the ravening killer.

"You sure it was him?"

"I'm sure."

Jhinn shrugged. "All I know is that he's only done good things around me. Only ever wanted to save people from harm."

As they rose over another wave a small fishing trawler came into view, the sail ripped and ragged, flapping in the wind. Burn marks scarred the sides of the boat and a hunk of wood was

6

missing from the bow, letting seawater pour into the larger craft.

"Ho!" a woman called from within the boat. At the sight of them, she scrambled up onto a bench, waving her arms above her head, her long grey hair wet and wild in the wind and spray. "Ho, there! If it's to the sea you take, turn back!"

Marielle glanced at Jhinn. His expression hadn't changed, his eyes still set forward.

"If you value your lives, turn back!" the woman called, while around her three others worked the oars. "We were fishing with five other boats on the shoals off the Fang when they came – a fleet of ships and not merchant ships as we see in summers, oh no! They call themselves *The Retribution* and we are the only ones who escaped their wrath!"

A breeze had stirred up, blowing into Marielle's face in a way that made it hard to catch the scent of the boat. She frowned, blind without her sense of scent.

"The Retribution?" This time, when Marielle glanced back Jhinn's face was pale. She could barely catch the worry of his scent – ochre and smoked paprika swelling into the air around him. "Queen Mer's Retribution?"

"The very same! No ship or boat shall be allowed to pass! We were warned to return to the land. We were consulting together when they attacked. We are the only ones who survived. If you value your lives, turn back!"

"Mer's spit!" Jhinn cursed, but he was already turning the gondola around, fighting not to be swamped by the rolling

7

swell as he worked his oar, the smell of fear swirling in his every movement.

Marielle swallowed, wiping her brow. She finally had a whiff of the people in the boat and it backed up the words of the people – fear in lightning blue and acid scent was laced with the sparkling silver and mint of truth. As they turned, she looked over her shoulder at the white sails in the distance. There would be no escape by sea. A fleet behind, a dragon ahead. They'd wasted two days on nothing.

"It will be faster when we aren't fighting the swell," Jhinn called. "Already, our speed picks up."

"Tamerlan needs a healer," Marielle said, despite the worry swirling in her belly. The wind was whipping up, stealing words from their mouths so that speaking was an effort but Tamerlan looked worse. His face was drained of all color and his breath appeared shallower. "If we can get him to Xin, perhaps we can find one."

She stopped to tend to him, letting the swell speed the boat forward as she placed her oar down and crouched over Tamerlan. She wiped his brow gently as his beautiful face screwed up with pain. He hadn't been conscious since their flight from Jingen City and if she didn't get him to a knowledgeable healer, he never would be conscious again. And then she'd never really know if he was a kind man to whom she owed everything or a horrific killer who would need to be put down like a rabid dog.

She picked up her oar again, pulling against the waves with Jhinn, letting worry tick through her like a clock tracking the moments of their lives. If only she could speed it up and get him to safety sooner.

## 2: Xin City

*MARIELLE*

The Cerulean River flashed blue and clear – as different from the Alabastru as two rivers could be. But here in the island city of Xin, the water was high. It raged around the cliffs and harbors were few.

Boats of every type and shape clogged the docks and moorings in a forest of masts and a jungle of seaside scents flashing white and blue and green across Marielle's senses in a way that was almost calming. Fish and trade wares, sailors and ship-owners, hard work, hopes and dreams, longing for home, sentimental memories, all the scents of a harbor tangled together in a tapestry of sea and sun and sand.

Pigeons flew in and out of the city from every direction. Marielle longed to read the messages they carried. Were there plans about what to do next now that the dragon had surfaced? News about survivors – maybe even about her mother? She felt a tug at her heart at the thought of Variena. She was a survivor. If she was alive, she would stay that way. And yet, Marielle felt a tug like she should be heading back to Jingen and sifting through the ruins looking for her. What if she was trapped somewhere? What if she needed help? No. Thinking like that would only drive her mad. She had to stick to what was at hand.

Refugees choked the entrances to the canal system of the city, waiting in long lines to be admitted through the city's locks, their small boats tattered and ragged and their occupants hunched desolately in the confines of their hulls, their eyes hollow and clinging and their scents black with despair.

Marielle tugged at her scarf, trying ineffectually to block out the black licorice whorls of their despair.

Jhinn watched the lines of refugees from a distance, his eyes narrow as if looking for something specific. Occasionally they would flick up to the sky, as if watching for the dragon to emerge again. He'd been like that for the past hour as they neared the island city while Marielle tried to get Tamerlan to drink something.

Every time he squinted she followed his gaze to where shapes of cloud and sky formed hints of dragon and she shuddered.

"Time," Tamerlan murmured. "He's getting free. Have to stop … time."

"How about if we work on that when you feel better?" Marielle said gently. He looked so young like this and so vulnerable. His height and broad shoulders seemed slight when he was stretched out in the boat, as if much of his physical strength came from the struggling spirit within.

He smelled – golden. Like himself. Warm honey, cinnamon, and sunshine laced with hints of strawberry and tarragon. She had grown used to the smell over the days at sea, but that didn't make it less potent. It still threatened to steal away her good sense if she let her self-control slip. She didn't dare do that. She didn't dare play with that kind of fire. Any girl who let herself obsess over a monster got the punishment she deserved.

And it didn't help that she couldn't tell if she were smelling him when she smelled that golden scent – or if it was her own attraction – or if it was something else. It was all such a terrible tangle, like boat lines left in the bottom of a ship. She'd watched sailors on the docks working for hours to free the tangles and knots that developed over time. Her emotions tangled with who Tamerlan was and with this insanely strong attraction she felt for him into a thing that seemed to have a life of its own. It was easiest to think of it simply as her own attraction. It was easiest to manage it that way – to shove it into the back of her mind and pretend she wasn't drunk on it whenever she was around him. It was worse than blood. Worse than magic.

But now Tamerlan's scent was also edged with corruption as the infection flared through it, curling the edges with hints of sickly green.

She turned up to Jhinn. "We will have to pick a place sometime, Jhinn. He needs help."

"Cool your head, sister," Jhinn growled. "I'm looking for something."

"You've been looking for an hour." Marielle tried to keep her tone mild, but irritation was slipping out.

The longer Jhinn waited for his perfect opening – whatever it was! – the longer Tamerlan suffered without help. He was so hot she could have boiled a kettle on him, his cheeks flushed and his brow pale. She'd seen fevers like this before. He was well past her ability to do anything for him.

And the sun setting meant another night in the boat with the cold of night adding to the clammy water in the hull and that would only make things worse.

The voices in the boats nearby were hushed and sedate – as if no one else hoped to make it into Xin tonight either. There were boats dotting the sea all around them as they worked their way toward Xin. Houseboats of the Waverunners, packed with their whole lives and families. Gondolas with water-soaked refugees and rafts of broken timbers and frayed ropes with people clinging to them for dear life.

With this many near Xin, Marielle couldn't even imagine how many would be along the jagged coastline between here and Jingen or flooding into Yan further up the Alabastru River. Anyone on foot would have headed to Yan. Likely, that city was as choked by refugees as this one was. But thank the Legends it was summer and not the depths of winter. But what would they do when the weather cooled and sleeping outside became life-threatening?

Out in the bay, the dark ship flying Lord Mythos's flag was at anchor along with merchant vessels and two of Xin's warships. They seemed unconcerned by the faraway white sails, as if a line of invaders hadn't emerged from the hazy horizon only two days ago. A little further out a ships' boat of a strange design was rolling in with the waves from far out at sea. Another fisherman, perhaps. Sent home by the fleet.

Tamerlan began to cough and she hurried to put down her oar and check him. Rasping, barking coughs shook him as his face whitened. This wasn't good.

She looked at the clogged locks and then back to where Jhinn piloted the boat. His lips drew a firm line and then they rocketed forward, weaving between boats and squeezing into cracks too small for a normal-sized craft.

Curses followed them, but Marielle clenched her jaw and ignored them.

"We all need shelter! Wait your turn!"

"What do you think you're doing?"

"Dragon's blood in a bowl!"

She steeled her expression, ignoring their anger and cursing. If Jhinn didn't hurry, she didn't think Tamerlan would survive. She held him down as he thrashed, trying to keep his arms tucked in so he didn't damage them in his agitated state.

Fear rolled off him in electric blue and acid scented waves, making Marielle's stomach roll and heave. And mixed in it all was a residue of magic – turquoise and gold flecked lilac and vanilla – that reminded her constantly of how he'd been injured in the first place. The residue should be gone by now, and yet it lingered and flared with his fever.

14

"Escaping," he muttered. "Escaping his binding. Coming free."

"It's okay," she murmured, gently wiping his brow. "You don't need to worry about that."

He muttered indistinctly and worry welled up in her. His golden scent that drew her in as strongly as a ship's cable and pulley – that scent wavered and flickered under his fever as if his life were flickering and uncertain.

"I can get you as far as the canals," Jhinn said as he continued his determined press through the crowds of boats, dodging swings of oars and the spittle of angry refugees. "But I'll have to leave you on edge. I can't go on land."

"Where will you go?" Marielle asked tightly.

"I don't know. Somewhere close. This is bound to settle down. I'll leave a message at the message tree – the closest one to this canal entrance."

Marielle looked up from Tamerlan, ripping her gaze away from his tormented features. They were in a lock, rising up with the water. Already? Jhinn had been faster than she could have hoped for. She ignored the angry glares around her. She could already smell their fury and envy, swirling up to her nose in gusts of green musk and garnet pitch. She'd smelled enough fury for a lifetime already.

"No better than the rest of us," a woman in ruined silks said from her gondola beside theirs.

"Yes. That's a good plan," she said, holding Tamerlan down again as his wracked coughs shook the gondola. He gasped a breath, seeming to choke on it before coughing again. Each cough tore at her heart. They should have come here first. They shouldn't have tried to flee for the sea.

"He had bags packed for himself and his sister," Jhinn said, pointing to the tiny trailing craft tied to his gondola. "They're stored in there. I'll give them to you."

Marielle nodded, scanning the canal as the door of the lock opened and they surged forward into the canal. There were three more locks above them before they'd reach the city. Could Tamerlan last even that long? Did she want him to? She still didn't know if she owed him everything, or if the world would be better if she let him die like this.

A moan escaped his lips and when she took his limp hand it was cold and clammy.

"Hold on," she soothed. He was innocent until she proved otherwise. She needed to remind herself of that. "Just hold on, Tamerlan."

What would she do when Jhinn dropped them off along a canal? She couldn't even lift him on her own. Maybe there would be coin in one of the bags. Maybe she could barter for help.

She tried to keep her voice confident and soothing as they rode through the clogged waters up the levels of locks into Xin. Her attention was focused completely on Tamerlan. Was it her imagination, or had his breathing grown fainter?

It was hard not to remember that only a few days ago he'd been an Alchemist's Apprentice. A shadowy quarry to her. A kind friend and good worker to those who knew him. And now what was he? Destroyer of cities? Killer of hundreds? And a broken, vulnerable man who looked like he was barely out of his teens, just now filling out in muscle and strength, the stubble on his jaw still short despite days without a razor.

She ran a hand through her hair. She owed it to him to save him, but she couldn't forget the people in the Temple District of Jingen that he'd slain. They'd been innocents. He had no reason to kill them. Had saving her made up for that? Should she really be fighting for his life?

The gondola hit something with a jarring bump and Marielle looked up. They'd reached the inside of the City of Xin. The Trade District was on one side of the canal, by the looks of things and they had landed against the Spice District. A steep wall of rock rose behind the District, climbing up to where another wall rose. The Temple and University Districts of Xin were up in those rocks. The city was laid out just like Jingen, but on a rocky, steep island instead of a broad muddy river plain.

People packed the edges of the canal like fish laid out for sale in a cart. There was barely room to press another body onto the canal ledge. Sounds filled the air, voices raised, people shouting to get each other's attention. The other side of the canal looked even worse. Refugees huddled in clumps – their ruined clothing a sign of their new station in life. Marielle caught a glimpse of City Watch uniforms as Watch Officers pressed through the people, demanding order. She clutched awkwardly at her tattered silk dress. She felt undressed in the foolish thing. A single glance at the guards made her long for a uniform again, but she shook her head. A foolish thought in a moment like this.

She tried to wind the scarf Jhinn had given her around her face one more time. There wasn't any more length left to wind around her face but the scents here were overwhelming and she needed to focus. Jhinn was already throwing a pair of jute bags onto the stone ledge. He hurried over to her, frowning at Tamerlan. After glancing around them he leaned in low.

"Watch out for the spirits that haunt him, okay? The one with the breastplate looks especially vengeful."

"What?" Marielle gasped. The witness reports in the Temple District had mentioned a woman in a breastplate, too. Some of the witnesses had thought Tamerlan was two people – a maniacal woman in armor and a young apprentice.

"The spirits. They won't leave him alone. They are here right now. They steal his choices and make him do things. Watch out for them." She stared at him, her mouth open and he shook his head. "You're going to help him, right? You're not going to stop because of spirits, right? If he hadn't brought you to me, you would be dead. You owe him."

Marielle pressed her lips firmly together before answering. "I know."

She leapt from the gondola to the stone ledge. She'd have to figure out what all of that meant later. Right now, she needed to find a healer.

With Jhinn's help — him reaching from the boat, and her standing on the shore — she pulled Tamerlan from the boat to the stone ledge, propping him against one of the jute bags. Jhinn grabbed her hand and pressed two coins into it.

"Do what you can. I will look for your message on the tree."

He pointed to a nearby pole, plastered with fluttering white missives, before turning his gondola and skimming away. Marielle stood up, slinging one of the bags over her shoulder, her eyes skimming the crowd looking for help as Tamerlan sagged against her knees.

For the first time in a long time, she felt lost.

# 3: HOODED HELP

*MARIELLE*

"Can I get some help, moving my friend?" Marielle asked a man as he passed by. His arms were empty, but he didn't even glance her way.

"I can pay!" she offered the next man, but he shoved her aside so roughly that she nearly fell into the canal. With a grimace, she hitched up her dress, glad she had fled Jingen in her City Watch boots instead of the slippers that Lord Mythos had given her.

The Spice District smelled of resentment – a mushroom and sepia smell that made her nose wrinkle – in fact, it smelled so strongly of smug resentment that she was barely catching whiffs of the thyme and saffron, lavender and cinnamon that she expected to smell. She sighed, turning to block the way of the next traveler, a woman in Spice Merchant clothing.

"Please, can you help me get my friend to a healer?" she asked. "I'm willing to pay."

"Stop blocking my way," the woman replied irritably. "Three days and I've had all the refugees that I can stomach already."

She pushed past Mariella as the light on the street above them flared to life. The shadows were thickening as dark descended and Marielle had a bad feeling that sleeping on the cold stones of the edge of the canal would be worse than staying in the gondola. She was already standing over Tamerlan to keep people from stepping on him – how much worse would the press of the crowd be in the dark?

A group of Timekeepers walked on the street above the canal lip, close enough to the railing to be easily seen. They walked in a tight knot, their braziers held high, the incense wafting off of them tickling her nose with hints of ylang-ylang.

"Help, please!" she called to them.

"Your troubles mean nothing, supplicant. They are only temporary. Time is eternal. Remember, you are nothing and everything. You are one with the eternal, one with the all."

"Could the all spare a moment to help me with my friend?" she asked, trying to keep the bite out of her tone.

"When you learn proper mindfulness, you will see no difference between your pain and joy, between want and plenty. And in that moment, you will no longer be desperate for anything," the Timekeeper said, turning his back on her.

Easy for him to say with his healthy body, clean clothing, and perfumed brazier. Harder for the rest of them.

Desperation filled the refugees she saw. That, and the licorice black of despair. She'd hoped for a little generosity or at least a willingness to do business. Instead, she found hard hearts and self-righteousness.

She sighed, wiping her brow and tugging Tamerlan closer to the stone wall. He coughed again. Each cough tugging at her heart and complicating her emotions. Was he really plagued by spirits like Jhinn thought? Could his crimes have been their fault?

She leaned over him, checking his forehead with her hand. Was it a good thing or a bad thing that the rage of fever had cooled? Her emotions around her were already tangled into enough of a mess. The thought of his death tangled them further.

"I'll help you."

She looked up at the hooded figure in black standing in front of her. That voice …

She froze. It couldn't be.

He pulled the hood back, his expression grim where it showed from under a bandaged wound around his temples.

"Marielle," he said.

"Lord Mythos," she breathed. "You survived!"

"Despite your best efforts," he agreed, but his tone wasn't bitter, only factual.

"I just wanted to live." Her voice was small in her ears. Could he even hear it in the middle of the jostling bodies pressing between them and all around them?

In the street above the march of soldier's feet thudded past.

"Let's talk about it after we get him to the healer you've been asking for. I know someone."

Her mouth fell open. *He* was offering to help them? What was the catch? How was he going to trap them?

She looked around as if she'd be able to see it.

He chuckled, flicking his cape so that it flared with the expression. "No trust, Marielle? That seems unfair. *I'm* not the one who destroyed Jingen."

She looked around desperately, hoping that no one had heard. Why was he on the canal ledge? And alone? There were no guard anywhere nearby. No Landholds. No one of station or power but him.

"Why would you help me?"

He leaned in close, his dark eyes glittering in the light of the street lamp. It made her breath catch and her heart beat faster – like a mouse in front of a serpent. "I told you, Marielle, I didn't want you to die. I just wanted to keep Jingen safe. And it's too late for that now, isn't it?"

"What are you doing out here on the docks?" She was glad that this time her voice wasn't shaking.

"Do you want me to answer that, or do you want to get help for your friend?" He reached down and lifted Tamerlan up by the shoulders. "You get his legs."

Marielle swallowed, slinging the second jute bag over her shoulder and then grabbing Tamerlan's legs. Even with Lord Mythos carrying most of the weight, Tamerlan was heavy. His head lolled against Lord Mythos' chest and the former ruler of Jingen frowned as he stalked backward along the canal.

"You haven't been dipping into more magic, have you, Marielle? I'm getting a feeling of a strong residue."

Her cheeks felt hot as she replied. "I think it's left over from the other night."

The Lord Mythos coughed uncomfortably and they walked in silence, each focused on their work as Lord Mythos led them up the steps to the streets above and then worked his way down the street and around a corner to a place where a stone building jutted out into the street, a wide sign hanging over it.

It was clearly an inn with a common room on the main floor, but it wasn't to the inn that he took her but to a small door in the building just next to it. It smelled of herbs and worry – a rainbow of scents buffing out in multicolored clouds and swirls from behind the closed door.

The strongman stationed outside the inn door watched them suspiciously.

"No room inside," he growled when he caught her eye. Her scarf slipped down to her chest as Lord Mythos shifted his grip on Tamerlan and she was forced to pivot to keep her grip on his legs. "And aren't you the pretty one. There might be room for refugees in my apartments."

"No need for a room – or your comments," Lord Mythos said easily, shifting awkwardly to keep Tamerlan up while he knocked on the other door.

"What is this place?" Marielle asked.

"Spellspinner's Cures. Belonging to Allegra Spellspinner. Trader of Spices. Dealer in Cures." He winked at her. Winked! Like they weren't mortal enemies. Like he hadn't almost slit her throat and spilled her blood over the spine of a dragon just two days ago.

The door opened, framing a woman in bright light. She was younger than Marielle had expected – late thirties perhaps, with a brisk manner and a simply cut dress of expensive cloth.

"Back so soon, Etienne?" she asked, flipping her dark hair behind her shoulder.

Etienne?! She was a friend of the ruler of Jingen?

"We have need of one of your cures, Cure Mistress." He pushed past her, and Marielle scrambled to follow without dropping Tamerlan's legs.

"Collecting followers already, Etienne?" the Cure Mistress asked. "These two seem the worse for wear. Who put a sword in this guard of yours?"

"I did," he replied crisply as they climbed the stairs.

Surprise puffed up from her in a startled raspberry cloud. Ha! She might be self-confident and the Mistress of Cures, but she hadn't seen that coming, had she? Marielle wasn't the only one that Etienne Velendark was blindsiding tonight.

The stairs were an iron framework over the store below. A long wooden counter spread across the main shop with paper bags and glass jars filled with herbs and spices along them. Salves and potions, creams and lotions – everything you would expect from an herbalist. Marielle could smell them all, threading through the air like a tapestry of scent color, painting a picture of a thriving business – and something else. Was that orrisleaf she smelled? And flagleaf? Flagleaf was contraband in all five cities. Allegra could lose this shop if she was caught by the authorities.

Marielle's nose wrinkled as they kept climbing. There was tea brewing above and a man waiting at the top of the stairs. He was carrying iron – she could smell that much. A sword, perhaps, or other weapon.

"Do you have a guard here?" she said quietly, shooting her eyes toward the top of the stairs.

"Darlyn," the Lord Mythos said with a nod.

"And one at the back door, too?" she asked. She could smell someone there smoking puffleaf. And she could smell suspicion floating off the Cure Mistress as she spoke. With the scarf down, maybe she hadn't realized that Marielle was a Scenter.

"Who is this girl, Etienne?" the way the Cure Mistress said the words made Marielle's back tinkle between her shoulder blades. Would the woman plant a knife there if she didn't like the answer? "Why is she commenting on my … associates?"

"One of my guards," Lord Mythos said easily. Which was true in a way. Because Marielle had been a Jingen City Guard before the dragon rose from beneath the city. And the Lord Mythos *was* Jingen.

The top of the stairs opened to a big loft under a vaulted ceiling of raw beams. Marielle could see where the clay tiles were secured to crisscrossing wooden slats and huge windows overlooked the Cerulean River and the ocean. She froze. Far in the distance, trails of smoke rose into the sky, spreading a dark haze across the land. She stared, paralyzed by the sight.

Lord Mythos cleared his throat. "Recognize Jingen, Marielle?"

She'd known it was gone, but her belly knotted at the sight as it finally hit her – there would be no going back to Jingen. Not ever.

# 4: Cure Mistress

*MARIELLE*

"Put him in the back," the Cure Mistress said briskly, tying a white apron over her silk dress. What a paradox. Was she a rich merchant or a hard-working cure-dealer? The eagle-eye she watched Etienne with suggested that there was more here than met the eye, though nothing in her scent spoke of anything other than sincerity.

Marielle followed Lord Mythos past the guard at the head of the stairs and through a tidy area filled with chairs and tables with small lamps and stacks of books to the back of the loft where four dark doors stood in a line. Lord Mythos chose the third door, leaning awkwardly with his shoulder to open it and they laid Tamerlan gently on the narrow bed. Marielle checked his forehead, running a hand across it, and trying to ignore the latent golden scent that hung over him, drawing her in with its hot honey scent.

"So, this is the one who caused all this trouble," Lord Mythos said.

Marielle gasped.

"Did you think I'd forgotten his face?" his smell was intelligent and dangerous – celery and birch smoke and … was that *rose*? Marielle barely bit back a gasp at that. "Or perhaps you Scent something more than I wanted to reveal."

His jaw clenched, the small muscle in the corner of the jaw jumping as it flexed.

Marielle looked away from the intensity of his gaze, opened the tops of the sacks she'd been carrying on her back and then setting the one with male clothing against the small washstand.

"Both of you out," the Cure Mistress said briskly as she entered the room.

"His name is Tamerlan," Marielle said, feeling suddenly vulnerable at the look of Tamerlan laid out and defenseless. It was as if her own happiness was dependent on his safety. She shook herself. What a foolish thought. Best to dislodge it immediately.

"It won't matter what his name is if I can't find him the right cure," the Cure Mistress said, pushing aside a small jar of flowers on the washstand and pulling herbs and powders from her apron pockets to replace them with. "I did say 'out', didn't I? Both of you out before I decide your credit doesn't extend this far."

She shot a warning look at Lord Mythos and he grabbed Marielle by the upper arms, steering her out of the room, and shutting the door behind them.

She gasped as they entered the large loft again, shaking slightly.

"Don't tell me I have so much effect over you, Marielle," Lord Mythos whispered and his breath on the back of her neck was a caress that made goosebumps run along her flesh. Not the caress of a lover – the caress of a snake, sliding around its victim.

"Of course not." She tried to scoff, but it was too hard. "It just feels familiar. The last time you held me this way you were about to slit my throat."

"Oh." He dropped her arms, clearing his throat. "Yes. Well, perhaps you've realized why that was so important."

"Yes," she breathed; her voice gone with her confidence. From the wide-open window, the smoke still rose, glowing in the darkness.

"Perhaps now you can see why I needed to kill you – even if I didn't want you dead."

"Yes."

"Perhaps you would like to know what you can do to make all of this right."

A stab of excitement shot through her. Make it right? Was that even possible? She'd give almost anything to make that happen. Almost? That was a lie. She would hold nothing back, not even her life if it could undo her mistake.

And yet.

And yet he was playing her like a four-string vitara.

She swallowed and swiveled, moving quickly to pin him to the wall with her hands. He leaned back, not resisting, his eyes widening slightly.

"Is this why you helped us, Lord Mythos?"

"Etienne."

"What?"

"Lord Mythos is a title – and one I no longer possess. You may call me what the rest of the world must know me as – Etienne Velendark."

"Is this why you helped us, Etienne? You want to use us for something?" her voice was low. "How did you survive the fall of the city? How did you find your way to the house of a healer and not to a palace? Why did you help me bring Tamerlan here? What are you paying the Cure Mistress? And why should I trust you?"

He laughed. "I like the bolder spirit. It suits you, Marielle. Are those all your questions?"

"No."

He quirked a single eyebrow.

"Why did you maneuver me into offering myself as a sacrifice on Summernight when you told me that you didn't want to kill me, and you already had the sacrifice you needed?"

"And is that all?"

"For now."

He smiled – a dark, wicked smile full of secrets and lies. And yet, his scent was open and honest – minty fresh. "Our world may have ended, Marielle, but with it, civility has not also died. Come with me and let us talk about it over tea while my friend attends to your friend."

Marielle swallowed, glancing at Tamerlan's door. Should she have trusted him to the Cure Mistress? What if this friend of Lord Mythos' let him die or even killed him on purpose?

Etienne leaned in, pushing her hands aside easily. "If I wanted him dead, I would have just kicked him into the canal."

Marielle's breath caught in her throat, but he grabbed her hand and pulled her after him.

"First," he said, "tea."

There was a small stove to the side of the big room and Etienne took a kettle from on top of the stove, pouring it into a waiting pot and placing it with cups on a tray before leading her through a door, up a twisting metal-lace staircase, and onto the roof. Marielle shivered at the view of the dark landscape beyond. The orange-tinged smoke of Jingen rose into the night sky like a banner proclaiming her sin.

"For a merchant, Allegra lives well, don't you think?" he said.

"I think I would like answers."

"So would I. Let's trade them, shall we? I will start with your most pressing question." He lit a fish-oil lamp, placing it on a small table beside where he'd set the tea and then he sat on a small bench, gesturing for Marielle to take a seat on the bench with him. She hesitated, waiting long moments before finally giving in. He poured their tea elegantly, like it was all he needed to do that day – like it was all he cared about. It smelled of jasmine just as he smelled of rising hope – bronze and morning dew and she could have sworn a tiny tinge of rose.

"Why you?" He looked at her through thick lashes, like he was trying to be seductive. If he was, it wasn't working. Marielle felt like a wren cornered by a cat. "Things change. Sometimes rapidly. Yes, we had a sacrifice, but the price for a bride is greater than the price for a sacrifice, and I owed the Lord of Yan a favor."

"Are you saying you were going to kill me and marry Amaryllis?" Marielle asked.

He chuckled. "No. Someone else is going to marry her. Someone to whom I owe a favor. I was only required to spare her life. But with that came the necessity of finding an alternate sacrifice – or watching my city destroyed by the dragon within."

Marielle shivered. "That was all supposed to be a legend."

"Who says that legends can't be true?"

"It was just a dusty old ceremony."

"Built on a violent truth, I'm afraid." He sounded sympathetic. Dark shadows hung over his narrow face, steeping him in mystery.

"You sound like you don't blame me."

"Oh, I don't," he said, sipping his tea delicately. "All things strive. All things try to live. This is the nature of reality. I expected that from you. Why do you think the chair had straps? I just didn't bet on *him*."

He looked at the floor beneath him toward where the Cure Mistress was working on Tamerlan.

"Why are you here?" Marielle asked.

"Oh no, Marielle, for every question I answer, you must answer one for me. Did you know that man would save you when you volunteered to be sacrificed?"

"No."

"Do you know who he is?"

"My turn, remember?" she said, sipping her own tea.

He waved a hand dismissively. "I am staying with Allegra because it is … convenient … for me not to be in the palace or with the Landholds. Allegra and I are old friends."

He was an old friend of a merchant and healer? He didn't think that was strange? Marielle longed to ask more, but she needed to be careful. She only had so many questions.

"Do you know who he is?" Etienne pressed again.

"Yes," Marielle said.

"And are you going to tell me?" he sounded impatient.

"I don't know if you can use it to hurt him."

34

"If I planned to hurt him, I already would have. I am a man of action – a man with fewer resources and less power, but still with the ability to kill a man on the brink of death." He smirked as if he was enjoying the irony. "In fact, if I had simply left you along the canal, nature would have taken its course and likely he would have died in the night. No one else was going to help you, Marielle. No one else dares to bring in refugees. The city is too clogged. The resources too stretched – and it is only two days since we arrived. Two days!"

The teacup slipped from his hand, clattering to the floor and with a curse, he dove for it.

Marielle's eyebrows rose. She'd never seen him so discomfited before.

"Before – in the base of the tower – you said you had access to power to defend the city."

The look he shot her was murder wrapped in silk. "Yes."

"So, can't you use that magic now? Can't you use that magic to restore Jingen?"

His laugh was bitter. "You stole that from me, Marielle. You stole my power with the breath of your lungs and the beat of your heart."

He was on his knees in front of her, picking up pieces of pottery and it felt strange to be looking down at such a powerful young man while he kneeled before her. His movements were quick and precise, like he had coiled springs inside and he was afraid to let them leap free. He looked up at her, his black eyes burning.

"You stole my city and you stole my life. You stole everything. Without the dragon chained beneath Jingen, I don't have enough magic left to light a candle. The dragon took everything from us. And now you are going to help me make it right." His velvet eyes burned in the night. "Forget all your other questions, because this question is the only one we need to concern ourselves with – how can we stop the dragon from returning and destroying the rest of the Dragonblood Plains?"

Marielle shivered. She'd been so concerned with surviving and with getting help for Tamerlan that she hadn't stopped to realize that killing the dragon was now her responsibility. After all, if she was responsible for setting him free, wasn't Etienne right that she was also responsible to bind him again?

She gazed into Etienne Velendark's eyes, looking for any sign of deception. They were wide, reflecting the bright light of the moon through the window and the flickers of the bright rising smoke in the distance and they looked so vulnerable from where he watched her on one knee. Certainty swirled around him in silver and mint, making everything it touched more powerful, stronger, brighter. And in the certainty, there bubbled up bursts of bronze hope like morning dew.

She swallowed, her mouth suddenly feeling dry. It felt strangely like making a vow or pledging her oath to a king – though it was him on one knee and not her – when she eventually spoke.

"I will help you destroy the dragon."

Etienne rose in one fluid motion, putting the pieces of pottery in a careful pile on the table.

"Then it is agreed. We'll speak more tomorrow. I think you can visit your friend now." He nodded toward the stairs leading back down to Tamerlan's room.

"His name is Tamerlan," Marielle said.

Etienne smiled as if she had given him a gift.

# 5: A MATTER OF DEBT

*MARIELLE*

Marielle woke with a start. She'd fallen asleep in the chair beside Tamerlan's bed. He was still now, his scent stronger than yesterday and his face angelic in the early morning light. Last night, he'd been writhing and moaning in pain, crying out so loudly that she'd chosen to sit with him instead of sleeping, holding his hand and stroking his brow.

No wonder he had looked so tormented. His dreams were probably haunted by his crimes. And yet, if Jhinn was to be believed, then that sweet smell of innocence – the smell of soft baby's breath and summer grass – pouring off him was true. If Jhinn was to be believed, then it was spirits who had committed those awful crimes and not the man before her.

She'd tried all night to reconcile the two things – that he was an innocent boy with a generous heart who had only wanted to save a sister and ended up saving Marielle instead – and that he was a monster who had slaughtered hundreds of people to get what he wanted. She couldn't bring the two together – and yet she couldn't think of him as only one or the other. When she thought of him as a monster, she could see only his innocent eyes pleading for her help in saving his sister. When she thought of him as innocent, she saw only the tear-stained faces of the bereft in the Temple District.

Allegra had come and gone quietly in the night. Giving Marielle fresh water to bathe Tamerlan's head or pouring new doses of her concoction down his throat. She changed his dressing every hour, her work quiet and methodical.

"Do you do this often? It must take time away from your mercantile," Marielle had said.

"I'm a competent woman. I can do more than one thing at a time," had been her sharp response. And she was certainly competent. But Marielle thought it went beyond that. Allegra smelled of royal blue and gardenia authority – a woman who dictated the lives of others, who pulled the strings of greater events. And she was a friend of Lord Mythos' and the person he was staying with as he fought to regain power – because whatever he said about fighting dragons, Marielle was certain that was only part of what he wanted. And if he was staying here, then Allegra must be a part of his ambitions.

Oddly, she had not been rumpled or yawning when she entered the room through the night – as if she hadn't slept at all in between checking on Tamerlan.

There had been no talk of payment, and that suggested that Lord Mythos was footing the bill for Tamerlan's care. And it also suggested that Allegra was doing this as part of some longer game she was playing with the former Lord of Jingen.

Which meant that now Marielle was in debt to Lord Mythos. And he'd already indicated how he wanted to be repaid – she needed to slay a dragon.

With a yawn, she pulled herself up from her stiff seat and released Tamerlan's hand. It was hard to do now that his scent was growing stronger again. It filled her mind so that she wanted to touch him – even when it just meant bathing his head or holding his hand. She had to fight that. Giving into it even for a moment could lead to infatuation – or worse, obsession. And Marielle Valenspear was an officer of the law. She was not a silly girl who could afford to become obsessed with a criminal.

She needed to get cleaned up, she thought, as she finally broke contact with Tamerlan. And she needed to plan. How was she going to do that when everything about her life was so uncertain? She'd lost her career, her friends, her possessions and her purpose in one fell swoop. She did not know if she wanted the injured man on the bed to live or to die. The thought of either filled her with dread. Worse, she was an arrow with no bow, a law bringer with no law, a scent with no source. She was not the kind of person who charted her own course, she was the kind who always served someone or something, and right now she had no one to serve.

No one should feel so lost.

She pulled her badge out of her boot, looking over it with shaking hands. It was worth nothing now.

The door creaked open and Allegra strode into the room, shoving a bundle of clothes at Marielle.

"Get cleaned up. You're a mess. There is water on the stand and the clothes are from Etienne. This man needs rest and you watching over him like a hen with one chick isn't helping."

Marielle looked through the stack of clothing. Lord Mythos had been thorough. The stack held everything from filmy underthings to heavy leather bracers. It wasn't her City Watch uniform, but the styling was similar. The scarf smelled of the mollusks used to dye it – suggesting it was probably red or purple. The straps and tailoring were very similar – so similar that they were very nearly regulation. Strange that he would have this available.

Allegra raised an eyebrow.

"Do you think he'll survive?" she asked, looking reluctantly at Tamerlan.

"Do you want him to?" the other woman asked. "Sometimes you look at him like a sleeping lover. At others, like the man you wish to sink in the sea."

"I want him to live," Marielle said, her face hot with a blush. Lovers? The thought! But even on her own tongue, she didn't know if it was a lie or the truth.

"He will. But he needs rest. Dress. Go and find Etienne. He says he has work for you. I will watch over this one."

"Tamerlan," Marielle said, and the way his name rolled off her tongue made Allegra smirk. But she didn't want to leave Tamerlan. Even if she couldn't decide what she felt about him.

"Go. Or I will double your bill."

"My bill?" So there would be a fee.

"You didn't think this was all free, did you?" Allegra said. Her eyes narrowed speculatively. "We'll discuss your payment later. I prefer to be paid in service – something only you can give."

She left Allegra reluctantly as the woman prepared to dress Tamerlan's wound again, returning to the room she'd been assigned.

Allegra's words were unnerving. What sort of service would she ask of Marielle? What of Tamerlan? Their skills were dangerous in the wrong hands.

And what was she taking from Lord Mythos to house him here? He claimed his magic was gone with the dragon. Was that really true?

The bed was made in the little room she'd been allowed, and the things inside untouched. There was water in the pitcher and a silver mirror over the basin. Marielle stripped off her shredded dress – shocked by how filthy it was – and hurriedly bathed, combing her long hair out before braiding it neatly out of the way and then dressing.

The clothing fit. That alone made her cheeks heat. How did Etienne … how did Lord Mythos know the exact fit for her? Why had he purchased these clothes? There were even a well-made cloak and a thick wooden baton. No bell, though. And no knife.

She had her own knife and she slipped the sheath from her leg to her belt, testing her draw to be sure she could quickly pull it from the sheath.

She fished out the badge and the scrap of paper from her boot – the one from Tamerlan's book that she'd saved all this time – and stashed them in the pouch on the belt, wiping her dirty boots off with the hem of her ruined dress. She felt good to be clothed. It made her feel less confused, less like crying, less like a refugee. And yet, that was still what she was, wasn't it? A ship without a sea. A bird without the wind.

A knock sounded at the door and she hurried to it, pulling it open to see Lord Mythos there with a satisfied look on his face.

"Happy Dawnwait, Marielle."

She'd forgotten that it was Dawnwait – the first day of purification before Dawnspell. It seemed wrong that life should go on, and that festivals should continue after their world had ended.

And yet they did.

Today, every house of the city would begin to turn itself upside down, cleaning every last item of the house, gathering up anything extra to give to the poor, eating the last of the food in the house before the fast began. And tomorrow they would fast for three days until the morning of Dawnspell when the new year would start – clean, fresh and with the promise of food and the regular rhythms of life beginning again. Summernight might be the end of the old year, but Dawnspell was the beginning of the new one.

For the refugees, the purge of Dawnwait meant there might be clothing and other used items given to them. But it would be a hungry next few days. Already exhausted and paupered, there would be no food given or made in all of the city. Marielle's belly rumbled at the thought.

"Happy Dawnwait, Etienne."

"You received the clothing I sent for you. Good. We need to leave at once."

"We?" she asked, a hand on one hip. "What are you paying Allegra for her services?"

He ignored her question. "You promised to help me kill this dragon, yes? You wanted to redeem yourself from the sin of ruining your people and killing thousands? Well, you will begin as serving as one of my guards. There is an announcement in the Government District square today, which I must attend. And we must check for messages on the message tree near the canal where I found you."

And Marielle needed to see if Jhinn had left a message for her. And she needed to see if there was some way she could repay Allegra without being in her debt. And she needed to watch for the dragon – perhaps, if she saw him in action again, she would see a way to defeat him.

She nodded.

"And Marielle?" Etienne said as he leaned in close. "Remember, as we walk through streets crowded with new beggars, that all of this was caused by you and by your friend. And it is only you who can fix it. You aren't serving me because I demand it. You are serving me because you owe more than you can ever repay."

She shivered as the scent of truth and certainty filled the room with his words.

# DAWNWAIT

# FIRST DAY
## OF
# DAWNSPELL

# 6: WHORLS AND MAPS

*MARIELLE*

He had been right that she could never repay her debt. Marielle's feet felt heavier with every step as they left Allegra's shop – Spellspinner's Cures, the sign proclaimed – and entered the streets below. The first day of Dawnwait had begun, as everyone prepared for Dawnspell – the dawning of the new year. Sweepers worked along the streets and men with barrows loaded with scraps pushed through the crowds with calls of "Make Way!" and "Dawnwait Cleaners!"

Hollow-eyed people shuffled along the streets – that's how Marielle could pick out the people she was responsible for. They stood idly or wandered with trailing steps, some clutching children or valuables, all with hollow eyes. And with every glance into their hollow eyes, Marielle felt more hollow as if she were trying to give a little of herself to each one of them and failing, failing, failing.

The stench of licorice despair curled around them, infecting the brighter spirits of the locals and even tinging the royal blue power of the gardenia-scented soldiers who marched through the city like they were planning to assault the local shops.

"Xin prepares for battle," Etienne murmured as the first group of soldiers passed.

"Battle with what?" Marielle asked.

He smirked, looking significantly toward the sky.

If he meant battle with the dragon, then that felt ridiculous. The dragon was the size of a city – the size of this city. Nothing that size could be brought down with swords and bows. And it was her fault that it was loose.

She clenched her jaw – feeling bad about the situation wouldn't change it. She needed to solve it. She needed to kill the dragon – if not with an army, then with something else.

Her gaze lifted upward every few minutes as she studied the sky, looking for the telltale silhouette that could appear at any moment. How did you kill a dragon? If his scales had been so thick they had built a city literally on top of him, that suggested they would be hard to penetrate. There had been that one fissure – the one that the Lady Sacrifice kept open with her blood. Would it still be there? Could they hurt him through that?

The bells of Xin called out the hour – a Dawnspell tradition. They would call out the hour every day from now until Dawnspell – a reminder of the time – a new time, a new year, a time to make changes.

Large brass bells along the city walls were the loudest, gonging the hours slowly, but with enough force to drown out the voices in the streets of the city.

Bells of all sizes rang. Smaller brass bells on chains hung over doors – a sign of observance – bells hung from gondola lanterns by wide ribbons, bells even threaded through belts or around necks or dangling from hats – tiny silver bells for adornment and reminder of the holiday that marked the passing of time, that honored Grandfather Timeless, the only one not affected by the ravages of that nameless force.

Marielle knew the old catechism that spoke of Dawnspell:

*And why do we celebrate the passing of Grandfather Timeless? Because the time is short, and the days are numbered like the ringing of hourly bells. Because we do not know how much time is left to us or if time will ravage us or treat us with kindness.*

And she remembered what her mother always said, with a rueful laugh, "Time, Marielle, is a woman's worst enemy. All others can be vanquished or negotiated with, but not time. In the end, time always wins."

But Marielle wasn't so sure about that. These days, it seemed that she was far more dangerous than time. She was a worse enemy to herself than the years could be.

She needed to shake out of this. No one would care about her self-pity and guilt.

She shook her head. She was supposed to be paying attention, sniffing the air, watching the Lord My- Etienne's back. It wasn't easy with the scents of the city so strong that she had to wrap her scarf four times around her mouth and nose. It was the despair that was the worst. The licorice, aniseed, thick black despair. It hung in the air like fog. And underneath it, the undercurrents were no better – there was the usual everyday feeling of a city at work, but there were other things, too – worry, nerves, uncertainty.

"Stay close, Marielle," Etienne said over his shoulder as they pushed onto the docks toward the message tree.

"News! Hear the city news! One copper!" a man was calling beside the tree. Etienne flipped him a coin and he smiled. "The army is looking for recruits. All able-bodied males and females who pass inspection will be paid one copper per day as salary." Lord Mythos made a motion with his hand and the man coughed and moved on. "Lady Saga bids all the people of Xin to this year's Dawnspell Hunt. The announcement is at noon in the Government District square. There are also sails on the horizon."

"Sails?" a man in the crowd asked. He was dressed as a wealthy merchant. The news caller pointed at the wooden bowl at his feet. News must be paid for.

Marielle searched the message tree as the coin clinked in the bowl and the news caller went on.

"Visitors from afar! But not merchants. They slew fishermen and sent their skeletons rowing back!"

A bit of embellishment there for his coin, but mostly true. Marielle's fingers sped down the lines of messages, looking for her name. Nothing. Nothing. She moved to the next branch.

"And the refugees?" a woman called. "Will Yan take their share?"

"Yan is choked with refugees. Many more went there than to Xin. It will be a hard year," the man called back as coin clinked into his bowl.

It would be harder for the refugees, but these people didn't seem to be thinking about that.

Her finger still sped along the messages. Nothing for her.

Frustrated, Marielle found the appropriate branch of the tree where it stuck out over the canal for access by gondola. She located the cluster of messages posted under "J" and carefully jammed her tiny roll of paper into the proper hole. If Jhinn stopped here, he could read it then. He hadn't left messages for her or Tamerlan. She hoped he was safe. Where would he have spent the night? He had food and water and even coin in his little boat, but he was just one young man in a hostile city.

"Who do the sails belong to?" someone in the crowd pressed the news caller again as Marielle pushed back through the crowd to where Etienne stood, his shoulders back and his head held high. He wasn't a large man, but his confidence made him seem larger than he was. So large that despite the press of bodies there was a clear ring around him.

He was watching the crowd, studying them as if gauging their reactions. Why did he bother? They were so easy to read that Marielle didn't even need to rely on scent. She could see their nervous expressions, their wary, closed-off eyes, and their firmly pressed lips. These were people at the edge of comfort, afraid that they were about to permanently drop off the side.

"Brigands and Thieves, no doubt!" someone said. "Pirates and scum who would never dare set foot in this city!"

There was the sound of cursing from further down the docks and Marielle stood on tiptoes as a scent she'd never smelled before drew her attention. Or *had* she smelled it before? There was something oddly familiar about it, like the sound of a song from infancy.

"Ghosts!" the news caller claimed. "The Dead come back among us!"

"We could destroy them all with a few fishing boats and a gondola," another man was saying boldly, the people around him adding their own jeers as he continued. "Show them – "

But his words were lost to Marielle. She was completely drawn by the scent of whoever – or whatever – was coming toward them. She could smell the distinct smell of magic – vanilla and lilac – but that wasn't all. There was a smell of salt, something floral that she couldn't identify, and something harsh and tangy that again was past her experience. She lost her balance. She'd tried to stand too tall and toppled slightly into Etienne.

"My apologies," she breathed, but her attention was still riveted toward that scent. She was waiting for a glimpse of who it was – and after a moment, she realized Etienne had not replied. He was waiting, too, his whole body leaning forward like a Scenter as he waited for their quarry to emerge.

An angry shout rang out from the direction of the eddy in the crowd and then something hurtled through the air. Marielle's baton was out before she even thought, batting the projectile away – an old shoe by the look of it – just before it collided with Etienne's head.

The crowd parted at the same instant to show five people unlike any she'd seen before.

Three of the five were bare to the waist, their skin so covered in dark green tattoos that it made it hard to make out the features beneath them. They were made up of whorls and what looked like maps – coastlines, islands, eddies in the sea, schools of fish. But no two of them matched, even though bits of coastline seemed to repeat across the three. These three carried harpoons, wickedly sharp with handles worn for use.

Marielle stiffened. Her baton would be no use against harpoons.

Someone from behind her threw a rotten rutabaga over her head at the strangers. A harpoon flashed out, spitting the rutabaga with ease. Was this really a city of the Dragonblood Plains? Reduced to throwing vegetables at strangers?

Her lips firmed. These strangers were not Jingen refugees, but they were visitors here – merchants, perhaps, from faraway lands – and in Jingen the City Watch would have put a stop to this by now. Where was the Watch? She scanned the crowd, catching a glimpse of a Watch Uniform as the officer melted into the crowd. Coward!

"It's them!" the news caller cried. "The visitors from the ships! The ghosts!"

The crowd around them pulled back at the same time that a half-rotted cabbage flew between the tattooed harpooners and toward the woman at the head of the group. She spun into a defensive leap, sword out and arcing through the morning light so quickly that Marielle hardly had time to gasp before the cabbage was sliced in two, the two halves falling harmlessly into the crowd.

There was a hiss of indrawn breath from the watchers. And no wonder. Marielle had never seen someone move so fast.

"They don't look like ghosts to me," Marielle said quietly.

The woman's face was pure fury, anger burning bright in a flushed face. Her hair was cut short except for a single long forelock at the front. A light-colored tattoo swept across her right cheek with writing Marielle did not know. Unlike the rough harpooners around her, she wore a high-necked, closely-tailored, dark coat that buttoned up the front in a double row of buttons. The coat flared where it reached her hips, widening over tight trousers and high black boots.

How did she move so quickly in such a tightly fitted coat? Marielle squinted as she studied the coat. Ah! There were slits cut along the sides and at the joints to allow fast movement without sacrificing the straight lines of the dark uniform. She felt a small smile form on her lips. It was a good uniform. The kind of uniform someone wore when they represented order and law. The owner of the coat had a scent of pure anger, hard as flint and just as deadly.

The man behind the woman with the sword was dressed in the same way, though with a loose scarf hanging around his neck patterned in a way similar to the writing across his left cheek – a tattoo of pale letters in a wave-shaped whorl. He was a head taller than Marielle was, twice her age, and the scars across his face – one even marring his tattoo – spoke of a hard life. He smelled of the mint of certainty.

Those harpoons looked promising. What if she tried to harpoon the dragon like a great oilfish in the sea? Perhaps these men were for hire. Perhaps, they could even teach her how to do it.

"You aren't welcome here!" the news caller yelled as the crowd turned toward the newcomers, leaning in.

Marielle scented the red of the mob beginning – the drive toward violence. She could feel it, electric in the air. One wrong word, one threatening action and people would die here. And where was the Watch? Where were they to stop this? She didn't see a uniform or badge in sight. If Captain Ironarm had been here she would have scathed them with her judgment. There were no cowards in the Jingen City Watch.

Etienne caught her eye, quirking an eyebrow as if he expected her to do something here. But what? This was not her city. She had no authority here! But then, neither did he, and he'd still managed to help her last night. Maybe it didn't matter that she didn't have the right to act. Maybe all that mattered was that she tried to uphold the law anyway.

She pulled her Jingen City Watch badge from her belt purse, hoping it looked enough like local ones to fool the crowd. She held it above her head as she spoke, dodging a clump of thrown mud as she bellowed.

"City Watch!" Did they notice that she hadn't said which city? "By order, you are to cease your attacks! Be about your business!"

Etienne nodded, not looking at her as he strode toward the woman with the sword, speaking quietly with her before pulling her after him. Her group followed him, hurrying toward the steps leading up to the next level of the Trade District.

"Return to your business citizens!" Marielle bellowed.

"No offense, officer!" the news caller said as Marielle hurried to follow Etienne. Where was he taking these strange visitors? Could they really be from the ships? "If I'd known it would disturb the peace, I would have stuck to happier news! Such as the good tidings that the son of the Lord of Yan will be delivering this year's Dawnspell Quest in the speech in the Government District today!" She was almost out of earshot when he added, "Both he and his lovely bride to be, Amaryllis Zi'fen!"

She spun, stunned for a moment before asking, "Who?"

# 7: A Sister's Price

*TAMERLAN*

Gulls calling from outside the open window were the first things that Tamerlan heard. His eyes popped open and he sucked in a long breath, looking at the white plaster ceiling above him. He could have sworn he would wake up in a gondola on the water – or not at all. The last thing he remembered was bleeding and pain, slumping in the small boat while the world fell apart around him. But here he was, back in the Alchemist's Guild.

*It's not a dream, pretty man.*

He gasped at the sound of Lila Cherrylock's voice in his mind. Oh no.

He sat up quickly – or tried to – moaning at the pain that shot through his shoulder at his sudden movement. He squeezed his eyes shut against it, shaking not just at the pain, but at the memories ricocheting through his mind. He shouldn't still be alive. He should have died in the fall of Jingen.

*But where would the fun be in that, pretty man?*

57

And the voice. Had he smoked recently?

*Oh, I don't possess you. These are only echoes.*

And behind her voice, he heard another voice rumbling, *Dragons! Dragons loose in the skies again! They must be stopped.*

He was going mad. That much was clear. He needed to get away from people before he caused any more harm. Flee the city. Go to the mountains, maybe.

Someone had left water and a thin broth on a stool beside the bed. He gulped it down hurriedly. He'd need the energy from it to get away.

He'd been stripped, but his clothing was hanging on pegs on the wall. And his old jute bag was in the corner. Perfect. That had a little of everything he might need.

Dressing was not as easy as he'd hoped. His arm hurt if he moved it at all – hurt so badly that he had to stop and wait to gather the energy to keep dressing. It took long minutes to slowly drag one article of clothing on at a time and he was breathless when he was finished.

*Best to fight through pain. Pain is temporary. Inaction lasts forever.*

That was Byron Bronzebow. He'd recognize those words even without the resonant voice behind them. There had to be some way to make the Legends all shut up.

*I don't think you can, pretty man. You're in too deep now.*

He sucked in a long breath between his teeth, shuffled his boots on, and grabbed the bag. If he was going insane, then he needed to leave. Now. Before he could ruin more lives.

The window was wide open and he paused, leaning on the ledge and looking out over the unfamiliar horizon. The ocean was very near – or at least an ocean bay, fading off into blue where the sea met sky and merged into one. And a river ran past, faster and clearer than the Alabastru had been. That must be the Cerulean. He'd read about it. Which made this place Xin – the island city. It was going to be harder to flee an island, but certainly not impossible.

Okay, time to climb down out the window.

*With a hurt shoulder? You* are *mad!*

Or he could just walk out the door. He leaned down over the ledge of the window, thinking about putting weight on his shoulder as he climbed down the wall.

*You can't even raise your hand above your waist. You definitely can't climb. And you shouldn't be escaping anyway. There are worse things in the world right now than your guilt.*

He was getting used to Lila's advice in his mind.

*Go to the door and peek out.*

*Dragon!* Ram moaned in the background, like it was the name of a lost love.

He peeked out into an empty room beyond.

*Walk out but keep an eye out for movement.*

59

There was the sound of footsteps nearby.

*Go in the door to your left.*

He slipped inside. It was a storeroom for herbs. Interesting. He could see some rare ones there, too. And was that flagleaf? He was tempted to grab a handful, but wasn't he already in enough trouble without adding theft to the list? He fingered one of the leaves, feeling the pattern on it.

*You're nervous about stealing a handful of leaves? I once stole a ruby crown with four rubies in it the size of your eyeballs. And that's nothing compared to what the Grandfather will steal if he gets loose.*

*I once stole the local Landhold's underthings,* Byron Bronzebow interjected, *and hung them from the flagpole to embarrass him.*

They were silenced by an ominous voice – one that hadn't spoken yet. *I've stolen the lives of thousands.*

And just like that, Maid Chaos stole away all the fun. He dropped the leaf on the floor and snuck out, slowly making his way across the broad loft to the spiraling metal staircase.

He should be worried about the voices in his head. But wasn't it normal to go mad after destroying everything you loved? He'd be crazy if he wasn't going crazy … right?

Voices drifted up from down below, hushed but brisk.

"Are you really going to let him stay here? Someone will want him dead and you might be killed in the attempt!"

"Who is mistress here, Danika? You or me? I will choose who stays with me as my guest, and I am not interested in your opinions on the matter."

"Will it affect the work of The Whisper?"

"Of course not. We'll just have to be more circumspect."

He stepped onto the stairs, being sure to make more noise than necessary. If they knew he'd been eavesdropping, they would not be happy. Those sounded like secrets. Except for the part about people wanting him dead. That was just a given, seeing as he'd ruined an entire city and the lives of everyone in it.

The stairs were terrible. Each step a fresh agony that tore through him like being stabbed all over again.

"On your feet again, I see," a woman said as he reached the floor of the store. That was definitely what this was. He'd been in and out of shops like these every day since becoming an apprentice.

"What is this place?" The glass jars held leaves and powders that he recognized. They were laid out in such tidy rows – and alphabetically. He felt the corners of his mouth twitching into a smile.

"Spellspinner's Cures. And see? You're cured." The woman's tone was dry and her dark hair was cropped at the shoulders in a blunt line. She wore a wide apron and worked at the counter, but Tamerlan thought it might be for show. Her cloth wiped the counter in a circle – not actually cleaning anything or polishing, just moving like she was pretending to work.

Quiet voices echoed from the back where storage was likely located under the loft, and two women in white aprons were carefully dusting glass jars behind her. No, she was definitely not just a spice merchant. He'd seen her type before. Guild Masters. She was powerful in her craft and she didn't just tend counters – or sick people.

The noises of the men in the back weren't casual with banter either. Even though he couldn't hear the words, the tones were sharp with purpose.

He gave her his best smile. "It seems I owe you a debt."

"It's being paid," she said with a smile that didn't reach her eyes. Ah. She saw him as a pawn. But she didn't think she needed him. She just needed the people she was using him against.

"How generous," he said with a smile. "By who, if I may ask?"

"A girl with dark hair who either wants to marry you or kill you. I haven't worked out which yet, but I have worked out how she's going to pay."

Marielle. Memories flashed through his mind of blurry glimpses of her face through fever dreams. Had she sat with him while he was ill? There was a comforting note to the memories.

"Well, a man's debts are his own," he said, smiling in a charming manner – or so he hoped. "Maybe there is a way I can settle the debt myself."

She smirked, eyeing him up and down. "There would be in any other circumstances, but not this time, I'm afraid."

She sounded almost regretful.

"And where can I find this dark-haired beauty?" he asked.

"Did I say she was beautiful?" Offense filled her dry tone. She sighed. "She'll be back tonight. She's staying here. Don't wander too far. Your shoulder will bleed if you put in too much effort and I need to finish the job I started if I'm going to collect payment."

She waved her fingers at him as if dismissing him.

"Where can I find the Libraries?" He wouldn't really go to the libraries, but it was a good idea to pretend he was doing something innocent, and not just running away from humanity.

"This city is laid out almost exactly the same as Jingen, except with different rock shapes and different canals. All the cities of the five plains are. Did you know where the Libraries were there?" Her answer was irritated, like he was wasting her time.

"Thank you."

He slipped out the door, hitching his bag on his shoulder and stepped into the streets of Xin. The bells were ringing the hour, a thousand peals of silver and brass in a cacophonous salute to Grandfather Timeless.

*And doesn't he crow about that during Dawnspell! A whole holiday dedicated just to him!* Byron sounded bitter.

Along the street, someone was sweeping. Dawnwait. He'd forgotten about the beginning-of-year celebration. The cleaning and fast were always crowded out by the excitement and revelry of Summernight. This year, he'd give anything to be able to clean the memories of *that* festival from his mind. If only it were as easy as sweeping the streets or hauling out the trash that had accumulated over the year.

Where was that dragon now? Was it still tormenting Jingen, or had it moved on to something else? Was it about to appear in the sky here?

He tensed, looking up.

*Dragon. Dragon. Dragon.*

Thanks, Ram.

"News for a coin! News!" someone was calling from around a street corner, and someone must have paid him because his words were chipper and loud enough for Tamerlan to hear.

"Renli Di'sham, son of the Lord of Yan is betrothed to wed Amaryllis Zi'fen, daughter of Landhold Zi'fen. Together, they will announce this year's Dawnspell Hunt in the Government District!"

He froze against the door of Spellspinner's Cures, his first thought one of relief – she'd survived! And his second one full of trepidation. His sister was about to marry the Lord of Yan's son. Had she agreed to that willingly? Perhaps, before he left Xin, he should pay a visit to the Government District. If she looked happy during the announcement, then he wouldn't have to worry. If she did not … if she gave any sign that she was being coerced … well, he had ways to deal with that.

*Yes!* Lila said in his mind. *Finally, some fun again.*

It wouldn't hurt anything just to check, would it?

# 8: Betrothed and Betrayed

*TAMERLAN*

It was harder to hike through the city than Tamerlan had expected. His wound flared with constant bursts of pain and he had to stop frequently to lean against a pole or rail just to catch his breath and stop the spinning of his head. He gritted his teeth against the nearly constant pain alerts as he climbed a long flight of stairs from the Spice District to the Government District.

Xin was a much more vertical place than Jingen had been, an island of rock and sudden spikes of granite – maybe. Or maybe not. Because if Jingen had been built on a dragon sleeping in mud, then wasn't Xin built on a dragon sleeping on the stone? Perhaps this stairway had been chiseled into rock-hard scales along the dragon's rib cage. Perhaps that explained why the stairway seemed to nestle between two ripples in the rock. Were they jutting ribs?

He paused for a moment, catching his breath, and turned to look behind him. From this high perch, it was easy to see the Spice and Trade districts of Xin perched on either side of the locks of the main canal. The rooftops – red tiled and beautiful – rolled out as far as the surrounding walls where small figures strode, alert and ready. There were more figures than he would have expected. Perhaps the local army was growing with the new dragon threat to defend against. Past them, the Cerulean flowed, and past that were the rolling plains that ended on a horizon plumed with smoke.

The sight of the smoke stole his breath away. His fault. All his fault. He'd done it for Amaryllis – and then she hadn't even needed his help. What hubris to think he was her only hope. What shocking pride.

But he'd saved Marielle. He barely knew her – only knew that she was dedicated to the law and that she'd showed compassion to him. Would he have risked everything for her if he'd known all along that she would be the victim of that ceremony? Probably not. And there was something wrong with a heart that would care enough to save a sister but turn a blind eye to the slaughter of a stranger, wasn't there?

If it was right to save Amaryllis, then it was right to save Marielle. Or it should have been.

There had to be some other way to imprison dragons than to build cities on them and pour blood over them once a year. There had to be.

*Dragon. Dragon. Dragon.*

Ram's constant mad ravings about dragons were rubbing off. Tamerlan found himself scanning the horizon for one and searching the rooftops for a hidden form. Where had the dragon gone? He was not here in Xin. Was he still ravaging Jingen?

What did dragons do other than eat and sleep?

*Kill!*

And kill.

What did snakes do? Weren't dragons just a kind of snake but with wings and magic and malevolence?

He scanned the soft blues and greens of the summer horizon before turning back to the sweaty work of climbing the stone stairs. It was nearly noon. Nearly time for the announcement. He needed a look at his sister. He could fight through the pain for that.

He tugged at the long blue cloak he wore. He should have left it at the healers. It was only making him hot and holding him back. He could shed it, but if he did, he'd have to carry it and his shoulder wasn't up to carrying anything.

Shed. Snakes shed their skins, didn't they? It was called molting. Perhaps that was where the dragon was. Perhaps the massive creature was up in the mountains somewhere, trying to shed the homes and roads and bridges built into his scales. That's what Tamerlan would do if he were a dragon.

He walked carefully through the dense crowd, barely noticing the people as thoughts of dragons filled his mind. The crowd was mostly dressed in white – the color for Dawnspell – except the refugees who had nothing else to wear. He would stand out as a refugee in his worn guard's uniform. He should remember that. But instead, all he could think of was dragons. How could he find out how to kill one?

His eyes drifted across the people as he crested the final stairs onto the cobblestone street beyond. A woman stood to the side of the pushing crowd, her eyes hollow, two grimy children clutched in her arms. Their eyes watched the crowd hungrily.

Tamerlan felt the blood rush to his cheeks and he patted his belt pouch. No coins. Nothing to give them. He glanced down at the silver cloak clasp with the palace insignia. That was worth something. Carefully, he pushed through the crowd wincing at every touch or jostle. He shouldn't be out of bed. He wasn't healed enough for what he was doing.

He had the pin out of the cloak and was handing it to the woman before he'd even reached her. Surprise widened her eyes. It shouldn't. Someone should have taken her in by now. How selfish were the people of this city that they hadn't? His face grew hotter. She reached for the pin but stopped before she touched it, as if she were afraid to take it. He shoved it into her outstretched hand.

"Take it. Feed your children," he said, his voice thick. On an impulse, he pulled off the cloak, offering it, too. One of the boys pointed wide-eyed at the sword on his hip. Without the cloak, it looked a bit too obvious, but he wouldn't change his mind. The way the woman shivered in the sea wind, she could use the cloak. And it was all he had to give.

"Thank you," she said, clutching the cloak and pin like they were treasures.

But he couldn't bear to look at her for a moment longer. She wouldn't be here if it weren't for him. She wouldn't be wondering how to feed her children.

Running away from all this wouldn't fix it – couldn't fix it. He only had one choice.

*Dragon. Kill the dragon.*

Yes, Ram.

He would have to kill the dragon. He would have to make sure there were no more refugees – and then if he were still alive, he would have to spend his whole life making things right – rebuilding, giving, serving. Running away right now – that wouldn't help anyone but himself.

With his cheeks burning and his wound on fire, he fled the refugee crowds, head down, desperate not to see or be seen. He felt something hot on his cheeks, but he didn't stop to brush away his tears until he was well into the Government District and down an alley, around a corner and then out beside a moat around a palace. He was so turned around that he wouldn't have known where his desperate flight had taken him if he hadn't seen the moat.

Roses climbed the walls of the palace and guards were ringed around the wall. From the calls and cheers, he thought that the crowd had gathered on the other side of the palace, waiting for the announcement. That's where he should be, instead of in this lonely street, far away from anything else. The buildings here were quiet, the moat still. Lily pads floated on the top of the water. He could smell the sun on them and their faint fragrance. But he couldn't bear to go to where the people were. He closed his eyes but all he saw in his mind were the faces of those children.

*Dragon. Dragon.*

A voice floated down from the palace wall.

"I thought that perhaps you would make the speech, my beauty. I shouldn't keep your charms all to myself."

There was a tinkling laugh. "I think that I'm starting to like you, Renli."

Amaryllis! Tamerlan stepped out, peering up at the figures on the top of the palace wall. They stood close together, as if their words were only for each other, though their voices carried easily in the clear summer air.

"Only starting?" he feigned a hurt tone.

Tamerlin shifted nervously. She sounded playful. She sounded like she wasn't being coerced. But she was only sixteen. She shouldn't be marrying at all – not yet. Although, better married than sold as a sacrifice. And he'd told himself that he would just check to be sure that she was okay. He wouldn't ruin things for her if she was well and safe. After all, it probably wouldn't help her any to be flirting with a future husband only to have her criminal brother storm into the moment demanding that she flee with him.

Tamerlan ran a hand over his tired face.

"I won't even know what to say!" Amaryllis protested, but she was clearly asking to be convinced.

"Just tell them about the hunt – tell them how we need to get rid of the dragon and how Abelmeyer's Eye is the only way to bind him. Tell them that it's a secret passed down from generation to generation."

Tamerlan froze. Was there really a way to bind a dragon with something as simple as a relic?

*Kill. Kill. Dragon.*

But Lila Cherrylock's voice pushed Ram's aside for a moment, *King Ablemeyer's Eye – an amulet – is what put them in those trances in the first place. It won't hold them for long – only blood can do that – but it could hold a dragon for a time. I would have stolen it if it wasn't already lost by my time.*

*You would have stolen it?* Byron broke in. *I would have stolen it first and used it for the freedom of the masses. Such a relic belongs to the people.*

Lost? How would something so precious be lost?

*Maybe it isn't lost. Maybe it was kept with King Abelmeyer's treasures. Who can say?* Lila suggested. *Perhaps the other Legends know. All I know is that it wasn't where I thought it would be.*

*You must join this hunt.* Byron was just as intent as she was.

Where did King Abelmeyer keep his treasures?

*Lila was first to answer. Hidden in the great works of art in the five cities. Or in the palace storerooms, but if it was in one of those, they would know, and there would be no hunt. You should open the Bridge of Legends and let me out. I want to find this treasure, too.*

That was too big of a risk. Tamerlan watched his sister and her suitor walk down the wall, away from him. Their voices faded away as they left. She didn't seem like someone who needed to be rescued. But this amulet showed promise. Perhaps it would be the key to redemption.

*Let me out and I will help you!* Lila insisted.

*Let me out and we will free the people once more!* Byron demanded. *Let us make payment for our sins.*

He'd have to do it without smoking. These Legends were far too excited at the prospect of this hunt. His hands trembled at that thought as if his body ached to dip into the Bridge of Legends again. But he didn't dare do that. If you let the Legends out to play, there was no telling what they might do.

*Kill! Kill them all!*

# 9: Windsniffer

*MARIELLE*

Lord Mythos seemed mesmerized by the woman in the double-breasted coat, but it was the man with the large conch shell who captured Marielle's attention. It glowed turquoise to her, though she couldn't tell what she was smelling when she looked at the shell, even though she sniffed hard, trying to catch the scent of it. It wasn't the turquoise of the sea or the turquoise and gold of magic – it was different than that, almost magical but not the magic she was used to. Stranger yet, even her eyes seemed to be seeing turquoise and that made her shiver at the strangeness of the experience.

Etienne had led the group to the inn beside Spellspinner's Cures – *The Grinning Cutlass.*

"No foreigners," the strongarm said before they even reached the door. Marielle flashed him a suspicious glare. He was the same one who had offered her a place in his bed the night before.

"An odd policy for an inn," Etienne said mildly.

"I said – " the strongarm didn't get to say anything else. Etienne's hand flashed out so quickly that Marielle couldn't see what he did and then the strongarm was leaning against the wall gasping for breath while Etienne opened the door for his guests.

Marielle was the last to enter, watching carefully for any trouble that might come from behind. This city needed a better City Watch. She hadn't seen a patrol yet and the few individuals she'd seen had scurried out of the way when trouble came. It made the hairs on the back of her neck rise up. A city without order was a city in trouble. Laws and order kept a place safe and prosperous. Failing to uphold them led to the kind of rot that destroyed a city.

Her lips formed a firm line of concern. No law. Refugees. A dragon threat. Xin was like a barge of dry wood sailing too close to a port light. The whole thing could go up in flames in a matter of moments. She would have to watch for that.

The inside of *The Grinning Cutlass* wafted with trails of yellow-orange and washing soda scent – greed and stone-gray suspicion.

By the time she entered, the innkeeper was already leading Lord Mythos to a back room. A woman with two pitchers, beaded with cool drops on the outside, followed the trail of foreigners.

Marielle peered at the customers, mentally cataloging them. Regular. Drunk. Two merchants eating lunch. Out of town visitors – older Landholds with business in the city. A suspicious character – petty thief perhaps? That dagger looked expensive for a man of that class.

She was only worried about the last in the list, but she fingered the handle of her dagger, sniffing the air.

His interest was piqued, little sizzles of electric blue excitement in his scent. She'd have to keep her eyes open or he'd pick their pockets as they left. If she'd been here with Carnelian, they would have scooped him up already.

Carnelian. Her last memory of her friend was that betrayal. She'd helped Lord Mythos drive Marielle toward that death chair. How had Etienne turned her loyalty? Or had he merely laid out for her the same thing he had for Marielle – that someone had to die, and it was better that it be Marielle than everyone else. Maybe Carnelian wasn't a traitor at all. Maybe she was a patriot? Most likely, she was just being practical. Carnelian had always been practical. Then why did it still sting to think of her?

She entered the room where Etienne and his guests were already arranged around the table where water was poured. Nothing else was allowed during Dawnwait. None of them were sitting, but they watched the serving girl and innkeeper like hawks until the two of them left. Marielle closed the door behind them and stood in front of it, playing the guard she'd promised to be.

"Who are you," the woman demanded the moment the door was shut.

"Etienne Valenspear, formerly the Lord Mythos of Jingen."

"The city that was burned three nights ago."

"The very same," he said, barely twitching at her words.

"And now you are here to welcome us to Xin – but you are not of Xin and have no authority here." She tilted her head to the side. Careful. Considering.

"You didn't seem to be receiving a better welcome," Etienne said. "And it occurs to me that we can work together. Please, sit and let us talk."

"We do not require your help." The woman's voice was terse.

No one had moved. No one had sat. And yet, Marielle felt the eyes of the man with the conch shell flicking over to her from time to time. He was curious about her. She could smell his interest, bright and fresh as cut citrus. It burst through the mistrust in the room in little marigold puffs.

"Then why are you in Xin?" Etienne asked. "Why send an advance team if you don't wish to talk – or to do something to prepare for the arrival of your people on the ships?"

There was a hiss of indrawn breath. "How did you know we came from the ships?"

Etienne raised a single eyebrow. "You don't rule a city of the Dragonblood Plains by ignorance and blindness."

"You aren't a ruler anymore." There was acid in her words. No wonder she hadn't found a warm reception here.

If she meant to insult him, it wasn't working. His smile remained steady, but it was Marielle who spoke up.

"You are the people of Queen Mer, aren't you? Like the Waverunners?"

The woman spat and around her, the men cursed quietly.

"The forsaken? Looking for their lost story? We are not such fools. We don't believe a single story will make sense of everything and bring peace to the world." Her fierce expression backed up her words, but Marielle tilted her head to the side, watching her. There was more to it than that. Her scent held contempt, but also guilt. Did they owe the Waverunners something? Or had they done something terrible to them? It was old guilt, bred in the bones, lingering still. Hmmm. She'd have to puzzle that out.

"Why not?" Marielle pressed.

"We don't look for stories," the woman said, standing a little straighter. "We create them."

Those were bold words, and Marielle liked them, but she was surprised when the man with the conch shell turned to Etienne and asked, "Who is the young Windsniffer? Is she of your ship?"

Etienne paused a moment before answering. "She is."

He turned to her, inclining his head slightly. "I am Anglarok of Ship White Peaks, of the Shard Islands of the Eighth Sea and I see my heart in you, young Windsniffer."

Marielle blushed. Windsniffer? Could that be like a Scenter? His nose wrinkled as she thought that. He was smelling her

78

emotions. She fought back a burst of surprise and replied awkwardly.

"I am Marielle Valenspear a Scenter for the Jingen City Watch."

"Have you a Wind Guide, Marielle?" he asked.

She shot a glance at Etienne. He shook his head almost imperceptibly. What did that mean? How should she answer? She opened her mouth, uncertain. It took her a moment to decide on simply answering with the truth.

"No." After all, she did not even know what that was.

He stepped away from the table, walking to where she was and circling her, seeming to study her from every angle, his nose wrinkling and sniffing constantly like a strange dog. Marielle shifted nervously, her belly quivering with nerves at the sudden attention.

"And I am Ki'squall Liandari of Ship White Peaks of the Beneficent Islands of the Sixth Sea," the woman said, "I am the Ki'Squall of the Harbingers of the Retribution. And in this city, I have found no welcome and no mercy and so we shall give no welcome and no mercy in the Retribution."

Her words sounded like a judgment. Marielle's blood froze with the pronouncement. It was laced with the scent of deep, royal-blue authority and a confidence so thick she could have used it to rig a sail.

"I've welcomed you," Etienne said. "And I would be pleased to help you with your – "

"We don't require help," Liandari said again. Anglarok clucked his tongue and for some reason, Liandari blushed. "They said there would be an announcement in the Government District. We traveled there to listen but were not admitted to the square."

"I can grant you access there," Etienne said. He sat down, even though the rest of them were still standing, and took a sip from his cup of water. "But surely you are not here to participate in Dawnspell."

"There was some talk of a hunt. A city-wide search for an ancient artifact," Liandari said carefully.

"There is always a hunt. This one should be as mundane as any other. The search for a simple trinket."

Liandari cocked her head slightly, as she seemed to do when working something out. "You are not so certain. You fear that this hunt will be for something that you actually need. You've asked them to make it about the mundane instead. You are waiting to see if your request has been granted."

Etienne smiled and Marielle couldn't decide if this was some sort of verbal duel or a meeting of like minds. "Would you like to come as my guest?"

"It will not wash away the insult Xin has shown us. It will not make this right." She crossed her arms over her chest, practically quivering with indignation. "We should be granted places in the palace as honored guests. We should be offered tribute and gifts. We should be begged for mercy."

"Perhaps it will be a start, yes?" Etienne asked affably, but there was an edge to his tone. He wasn't the begging kind.

Memories of the rows of white sails flashed across Marielle's memory. If that fleet was here to attack, could Xin survive such a conflict? What about right now when they were choked with refugees and under the threat of a dragon? She didn't think so. Maybe someone should be begging for mercy.

"What is the Retribution?" she asked and both Etienne and Liandari looked at her with surprise as if they had forgotten that anyone else in the room could speak.

Liandari cleared her throat. "The Retribution brings Queen Mer's justice to the land. As our prophecy says,

*A key will unlock Queen Mer's justice – the opening of a dam, the loosing of a river.*

*A key will unlock her children's glory – a changing of the tide, a babble of many waters.*

*Look for the key when the tides foam red and the dragons rise again.*

*Look for the key when the Legends walk the world of men and the shells sing a new song.*

*Look for the key in the blood of the dragon, in the dreams of the dragon, in the song of the dragon.*

*Look for the key in the smoke of the dragon, in the death of the dragon, in the shards of the dragon.*"

She cleared her throat before continuing. "We are the Harbingers of the Retribution – the first tentacles feeling the land before we seize it. We have come looking for the key."

Marielle shivered. If she found any keys, she would know exactly who *not* to give them to.

Behind her, Anglarok chucked, smelling of apricot satisfaction. "I like this one. She cares only about truth and justice. I will be her Wind Guide."

Marielle swallowed. As if things weren't complicated enough, now she had to find out what a Wind Guide was and what price she would need to pay to yet another creditor.

# 10: THE HUNT

*MARIELLE*

The crowd surged around them so powerfully that Marielle was almost pushed into the moat. She leaned her shoulder forward, bracing herself against the push of the crowd.

True to his word, Lord Mythos had brought them past the Government District guards to the very front of the crowd as the noon announcement was about to be made. He stood side by side with Liandari, pressed against the moat of the Palace. Landholds and important merchants angrily pressed in from behind them to regain their usurped position.

Etienne and Liandari didn't care. They stood like two islands in an ocean storm, untouched as the harpooner guards and Marielle watched their backs.

"Watch it!"

"Foreigners!"

The mutters and curses around them were not friendly.

Marielle's scarf was wrapped four times around her mouth and nose and even that wasn't enough to block out the green bursts of envy and sepia resentment. She missed Carnelian. Carnelian would have pushed people back, barking at them to make a path for her Scenter. Instead, Marielle was nearly in the moat as she tried to catch a fresh breath of air and not be overwhelmed by the scents of the crowd.

Normal scents were bad enough – freshly baked bread, fish from the docks, tanners, alchemists, spice merchants, and the thousand other every-day scents that clung to the people as they crowded together. But threaded through that was the anticipation of the hunt, swirling light blue and bright red with expectation and sweet-apple delight, and the undertone of ochre and paprika worry. There were also the beginning plumes of rose-colored obsession, and that worried Marielle. Whatever this crowd began to hunt for was going to be taken very seriously indeed.

"Make way for the Timekeepers! Make way!" a crier called, and the crowd pressed back, pushing Marielle even closer to the tepid canal water as the white-robed time priests pushed forward, swinging their gold and silver mandalas and ringing silver bells. Only a week ago, Marielle would have ignored them – just another religion with strange beliefs – but after the rise of the dragon, she didn't feel the same way. What if they were right about things, too? What if Grandfather Timeless was real? What if all really was one and one was all, and her past sins meant nothing because they accomplished nothing? What if all human suffering meant nothing because they were all just part of one greater whole?

She shivered. If the horrors she had caused meant nothing, then good meant nothing either. What a terrifying thought.

"Marielle!" a hand caught at her sleeve and she almost lost her balance into the canal. She had to drop into a crouch to avoid being pulled into the water. "Marielle!"

"Jhinn!" He was in his small gondola, clinging to the side of the moat. "How did you get in there?"

"I have my ways," he said, bright eyes sparkling. "Tamerlan?"

"Healing and safe," she said, glancing around to be sure they weren't caught, but no one was looking. All eyes were on the palace wall where a group of Landholds was assembling – Lady Saga the ruler of the city and her guests.

"And you?" he asked.

"I'm with them." Marielle pointed to Etienne and the Harbingers.

Jhinn hissed in a gasp and then the bells were ringing. So many bells of so many sizes that Marielle could hear nothing else over the tinkling and gonging and bonging filling the square.

When, at long last, they stopped, her ears were still ringing.

"Marielle, they're dangerous!" Jhinn warned, pulling her closer to him so she could hear his desperate words. "We need to get upstream and away from them. I've found out who they are and what they want."

"Some kind of justice," Marielle said, her eyes drifting up to where Lady Saga was welcoming the crowd.

"This Dawnspell marks a legendary hunt that will determine the future of our city!" Lady Saga proclaimed, her high-collared dress looking as well-made and carefully-tailored as Lord Mythos' jackets always had been. Like him, she was ringed with guards. "And for this hunt, the prize is like none other. A handful of gold might pay for a new shop or a freshly painted gondola. An invitation to a party might get you new connections or an experience you've never had before. I'm offering you something more- a single wish. If the item you are hunting for is found, I will grant the finder any one thing that is in my power to grant. So, search hard and make me proud!"

Marielle glanced at Etienne. He stood leaning forward, his jaw clenched and fists balled at his side as if he could barely control himself as the next speakers walked forward. Was that worry pouring off of him in ochre waves?

The girl with the long hair joining Lady Saga on the wide balcony made Marielle gasp. She looked like Tamerlan – soft where he was hard, slight where he was broad – but her likeness to him was remarkable. That was his light hair, his distinct jawline, his dreamy eyes. She even had shoulders a little too broad for her clinging dress – like his broad shoulders. Could that be his sister? It was strange to see her, knowing that she was at the root of all the tragedy in the past two weeks. She probably didn't even know it.

"It's worse than that, Marielle," Jhinn hissed as the newcomers arranged themselves. "They are coming to destroy us all. Beware any connections they make to you. They might seem helpful or benign, but any tie at all will bind you to them and you will not be able to escape. Promise me that you won't let them offer you anything!"

Marielle turned to him. "It's too late. The one in the button up coat has decided to be my Wind Guide – whatever that is."

"Mer's spit!"

But his next words were washed away by the announcement.

"I am Renli Di'sham and this is my beloved fiancé Amaryllis Zi'fen. Amaryllis will tell you about the hunt this year!"

"Whatever you do, Marielle, don't take any gifts from them, okay? Nothing, no matter how valuable, is worth that cost," Jhinn hissed.

"Okay," she said uncertainly. "What do you mean by that?"

But he was already rowing away as Amaryllis spoke to the noisy crowd. Marielle clenched her jaw in frustration.

"The Dawnspell hunt this year will be for King Abelmeyer's Eye," Amaryllis proclaimed. "A ruby amulet of great power. With it, we will overthrow the dragon which destroyed our neighboring city and we will make Xin safe again!"

A cheer erupted from the crowd – a cheer so loud that Marielle clamped her hands over her ears.

"Look for it in the hiding places of King Abelmeyer! Search his statues and drink houses. Comb his bridges and obelisks. We will find it somewhere in our city!"

There was a roar of approval and then Lord Mythos was pushing through the crowd. He grabbed Marielle by the collar, dragging her close so he could shout into her ear over the noise of the crowd. His eyes – desperate – were nothing compared to the pulsing orange and ginger of his scent.

"Take the guests to Spellspinner's Cures. I will return when I can. Keep them safe."

He was gone, slipping into the crowd faster than an eel through water. Marielle turned to the Harbingers, ignoring the fury on Liandari's face. Anglarok's mouth and nose were wrapped in a scarf just like hers, so she couldn't see what his expression was as she spoke.

"I've been ordered to guide you," she yelled over the cacophony. "Will you follow me, please?"

A knot was forming in her stomach. Jhinn's warning had been clear – she should be avoiding these people. But she had also promised to serve the Lord Mythos and she couldn't obey both at once. Where had he disappeared to? And why did he seem so shaken by the hunt for King Abelmeyer's Eye?

"I don't think your friend got his wish," Anglarok said as they pushed a path through the crowd for the others. "But don't worry, Windsniffer, when we reach our destination, I have a gift for you."

And how, exactly, was she going to avoid receiving it? Things just kept getting more and more complicated. Marielle felt a twitch beginning in the corner of her eye.

# 11: AT HOME IN A LIBRARY

Tamerlan gasped, leaning against the wall to try to clear the stars from his vision. What he needed was a glass of cold water and some sleep. What he wanted were answers.

The way forward seemed surprisingly clear and he didn't want to lose that clarity. Not when it might make redemption a possibility.

*The past can't be redeemed. But the future can be stolen.*

Lila Cherrylocks had a grim outlook on his chances, but she'd sing a different tune when he found a way to atone for his past.

This Library reminded him gut-wrenchingly of the Queen Mer library. It was Dedicated to Deathless Pirate, an ensemble of skulls and bones, shipwrecks, and artfully depicted crashing waves. And just like the Queen Mer Library, The Deathless Pirate Library was guarded by a pair of vigilant librarians, complete in long, smooth aprons with soft cloth gloves on their hands. They were as concerned with keeping finger oils

89

off parchment as they were with keeping humans away from their books entirely.

He wasn't known here. He didn't work for a guild or have a sponsor. And that meant his only hope of accessing the books would be to sneak into the library. With a wound in his shoulder that had been infected and was only just now recovering, that wasn't going to be easy. He took a long breath, flinching from the pain of it.

*Don't let them see you.*

Yes, great advice. Don't let the people you are hiding from see you.

*Your cynicism and selfishness will be your downfall.* That was Byron Bronzebow. *True heroes are men of valor both in action and thought.*

So, don't be selfish and don't let them see you. Got it.

*And don't take that tone with us!* Lila snapped. *Just do as I say. Wait.*

He waited. Waiting was good. It let him catch his breath.

*Pick up a small stone from that crack in the masonry.*

He picked it up.

*Think you can toss it past the Librarians so that they go to check on the books behind them?*

Probably.

*Do it.*

He grabbed the tiny stone, throwing it deftly through the open main doors and to the library beyond and then dodging back to his place against the wall beside the door. His wound flared with pain and he felt a seep of fluid in his shoulder. Great. He was bleeding again.

"What was that?" one of the Librarians asked and then there was the sound of feet on marble.

He peeked around the corner. The other Librarian was writing in her ledger, the *scritch, scritch* of the quill a steady sound.

*Get low.*

He couldn't crawl, not with his shoulder the way it was.

*Do your best.*

He stayed low, following Lila's directions as she led him through the doors and past the librarian's desk to the library beyond.

Simple.

*And yet you couldn't have done it without me.*

He really couldn't.

*Why are you here?*

To look for any information on King Abelmeyer. I need to find that amulet!

He angled his steps to hug the library wall, careful not to rub against the soaring bookshelves. That other librarian was in here somewhere and he didn't want to be caught by her.

*A waste of time. Abelmeyer may have owned the amulet and it may have been named after him as 'Abelmeyer's Eye' but you don't really think that it stayed with him, do you? You don't really think it's on a statue somewhere or in King Abelmeyer's grave.*

Why wouldn't it be? He was slinking along a shelf of Dragonblood Plain history. There would be something here about the Eye. If Tamerlan was at home anywhere, it was in libraries. His fingers skimmed the spines of familiar titles.

*Legends of the Five Cities*

*Power, War, and Inter-City Skirmishes of the Early Years*

*Tombs, Graves, and Markers*

He pulled that one off the shelf, carefully flipping the edges of the pages, careful not to damage them.

*If you are really adamant about finding this thing, you should just ask us.*

Okay, I'm asking. Where is it?

He skimmed along the book. The author had noted every tomb and grave by the name of the deceased. King Abelmeyer's was a huge barrow on the edge of the cliffs outside the city wall. It should be easy enough to find, though he'd have to dig to get into it. Oh. But there was also a sarcophagus in the city. Well, which one was he buried in, then? And why have two gravesites? The text tangled around the subject as if it was afraid to disclose the truth.

*Well, I don't know where it is,* Lila admitted as he searched through the text, *but one of the other Legends will. It's almost certain that one of us knows. Maybe even King Abelmeyer.*

*I don't know where this amulet lies,* Byron Bronzebow added. *But if you find it, you must not keep it for yourself. Wealth is meant to be redistributed to the people.*

He'd have to find it first. He'd worry about how to use it to bind dragons and help people after that.

*So, smoke your herbs and call the Legends,* Lila urged. *Someone will know where it is.*

*Dragon. Dragon. Dragon.* Ram sounded heartbroken as he continued his endless chant. It was giving Tamerlan a headache.

And what? Let them destroy Xin, too? Let them slaughter innocents and destroy the peace?

*Don't blame all of that on us. Ram only wants to kill dragons. And that's what he would have done if you hadn't called him right before a blood sacrifice! Any fool would have known that he had to stop that. You can't kill dragons and feed them at the same time.*

*Dragon! Kill!*

Well, *Tamerlan* hadn't known. And what other little peccadillos might the other Legends have if he called on them? Would King Abelmeyer turn out to be a conquering General who started a war? Would Deathless Pirate steal a ship and sail off to sea? Would Grandfather Timeless stop the passage of time and freeze them all in place? Who could say? And because Tamerlan couldn't say, he certainly wouldn't risk it. Not again.

Waves of pain crashed over him and nausea crept up. He'd better wrap this up and get back to Spellspinner's Cures.

93

On a whim, he searched out the next entry about a Legend.

*Deathless Pirate is said to be buried off the Dragon's Spit point. His corpse was never recovered from the golden cage he was locked in. They sank the cage off the point in the middle of a storm so that no one would ever be able to find that precise location again. Or so it is said.*

Helpful.

He was skimming to the next page when he heard a footstep behind him. He ducked and felt a whoosh of air over his head before he stumbled, nearly falling to the ground. The book was dragged from his hands as he fell to one knee, coughing and clutching his chest.

"Fools, all of them. And you're a fool, too," a quiet voice said in a menacing tone. The owner of the voice was agitated, his grumble turning to a rant as he spoke. "I told her not to use this as a way to find the amulet. I asked her to promise. And what does she do? The opposite! And now we'll have fools at every turn! And I told Allegra to keep *you* in bed and what does she do but let you out to bleed to death in the streets!"

"We're not in the streets." Tamerlan struggled to his feet, still gasping, his eyes widening as he saw the man in front of him. Lord Mythos! The ruler of Jingen! The man who had tried to kill Marielle and who had stabbed him through the chest!

He choked on his breath as he tried to form the words to vent his wrath, but the other man just chuckled wryly.

"Didn't expect to see me again, did you?"

"You're alive!"

94

"I'm hard to kill," Lord Mythos said, examining the book he'd snatched from Tamerlan. "And you are reading a book about graves. Thinking of designing your own?"

He raised a quizzical eyebrow.

"No," Tamerlan said mildly, but his mind was buzzing like a hive of bees. "What are you going to do now that you're here? Are you going to make trouble for my sister?"

"What does that matter to you, magic thief?" Lord Mythos said and Tamerlan's eyebrows rose as crossed his arms over his chest. He was a foot shorter than Tamerlan, but Tamerlan still remembered how quick he was with his sword and the way he was standing suggested that he might draw at any moment.

"I never stole magic. A grimoire, yes. Marielle, yes. People's lives ... I stole those." Tamerlan felt his voice growing heavier with each admission.

"My city," Lord Myths growled through clenched teeth. "My people. My dragon. You stole those! I can still sense the magic on you! You took it and you used it to destroy everything that I loved."

"Then kill me," Tamerlan said, feeling the blood drain from his face. "I won't deny any of it. I did all those things. I deserve death." He paused, letting his words sink in. "Kill me."

He spread his arms out, flinching from the pain in his shoulder. He wouldn't run from his fate.

"If I planned to kill you, boy," Boy? He was barely older than Tamerlan! "You'd already be dead. No, what I want is answers.

I want to know how you gathered the magic you used. I want to know where it came from and how to get it back."

Tamerlan hissed. "Some secrets are too precious to part with."

The Lord Mythos frowned. "Everyone has their price. Yours is the sister, yes?"

Tamerlan clenched his jaw.

"We'll work on the price later." Lord Mythos flipped open the book to the page that Tamerlan had been reading. "Deathless Pirate? King Abelmeyer? Hmmm. You are joining the hunt. Think you're up for it?"

He looked pointedly at Tamerlan's shoulder.

"I'll do what I must," Tamerlan said. He wasn't up for it. He wasn't up for any of this, but it was up to him to make it right. He had a debt too heavy to bear, a price too steep to pay. He'd just have to do what he could and hope it somehow sufficed.

"Your sister is betrothed to Renli of Yan," Lord Mythos said, considering Tamerlan. "But not everyone in Xin approves of Yan. And both cities are in a precarious position. With refugees flooding in – my people, now destitute because of your recklessness – and ships on the horizon, and harvest coming soon, there are many avenues for the more … ambitious … among us to plant doubts or sow chaos. And if they do – if there is an uprising or a revolution – she would be collateral damage. You went to a lot of trouble to keep her from me in Jingen. What kind of trouble would you go to for her safety here in Xin?"

Tamerlan ground his teeth. He knew a threat when he heard one. And he knew that Lord Mythos planned to use him. But what did he want to use him for?

"I'll do what I must," Tamerlan said thickly. But what would he do if he had to choose between redemption and his sister? It would be like making the same choice a second time around. Had he chosen the wrong path last time? He thought so. But would be able to choose differently? Did he have that kind of betrayal in his heart?

"That's good to hear. Because if you want things to remain stable, and if you want her to live, then you will have to help me."

"Help you do what?" Tamerlan felt like he was balancing on the edge of a knife as he awaited the reply.

"Help me find Ablemeyer's Eye before this whole city tears itself to pieces."

# 12: Chaos Bubbles

*MARIELLE*

"This way!" Marielle led the way through the Government District toward a massive stairway that would take them down to the Spice District below. She was almost at the head of the stairs when strong arms grabbed her, pulling her from the surging crowd and dragging her against a nearby wall.

"She's a Scenter! Look at that scarf!" He was a big man, twice her size. She fought for her knife, but her arms were pinned to the wall.

"The City Watch isn't going to help us find the Eye," his companion said – a smaller man and soft around the middle.

"She's not City Watch. She's not wearing a badge. She'll help us whether she wants to or not. Won't you little woman?"

Marielle spat, her belly clenching at the thought of being forced to scent for these two men. If they handled her so roughly in public, what would they do when no one was watching?

The man slapped her with his meaty palm, leaving her blinking at the stars filling her vision.

He growled, "We can – "

His head flicked from his shoulders so quickly that Marielle barely had a chance to gasp as blood sprayed across her scarf and clothing. The head made a heavy sound as it hit the cobbles and then the grip on her arms were gone and she was sliding across the wall to avoid his tumbling corpse.

She looked up, her jaw falling open at the sight of Liandari casually flicking blood off the end of her blade. Her single forelock of hair was slightly askew and she carefully stoked it back into place.

"You said something about following you?" She tilted her head to the side, inquiring as a pair of harpoons jammed through the smaller man's neck.

Marielle gasped, her eyes scanning the crowd for the City Watch. If this was her beat, she and Carnelian would have all of them in the hurry-up wagon before they could jab another harpoon. But no one was watching. Everyone seemed suddenly very intent on their own business, the scent of fear sizzling in lightning blue around their hurrying steps.

"You can't just kill people in the streets!" she protested.

"We just did," Liandari said. "Wouldn't your Windsniffer find them and bring them to justice if I had not?"

Marielle's gaze flicked to Anglarok. His scarf was wrapped around his face, obscuring his expression. Windsniffer. He was just like her. He didn't just sniff the wind, he also pursued injustice.

"Yes," she said a little breathlessly.

"Then we have no problem here. Lead on."

Marielle clenched her jaw and hurried through the crowd, ignoring the furtive stares of the people around her. Fear flickered along the edges of the crowd in lightning blue sizzles, but there was more than that. There was a deep throbbing yellow-orange greed, scalding her nose like washing soda. And there was more than one person looking at her with a rusty scent rising up from them. They wanted her ability. They thought it could help them find the Eye.

Marielle quickened her pace. It would be better not to be anywhere near the crowd right now. Even with six deadly warriors at her back.

By the time they arrived back at Spellspinner's Cures, Marielle was holding her breath. The scent was too much, even with the scarf wrapped around her head four times. She burst into the shop, gasping for breath as she walked into the clean room.

Dust hung in the air from a recent sweeping, but a young woman was furiously scrubbing the floor and calming the dust. Another pair of women worked on the windows, carefully polishing the glass. Marielle had almost forgotten about Dawnwait, but the calm of their concentration – jasmine in slate grey puffs – soothed her. There was a faint whiff of something else, too, but in the natural scents of the cures in the back of the shop, the scent was overpowered. Hmmm. A puzzle for another time.

"What is this place? I thought you were taking us to the inn?" Anglarok said at the same moment that Allegra bustled in.

"What's the meaning of this, Marielle? We are not a hostel."

"Etienne sent them," Marielle said, still gasping breaths of relief to soothe her scalded lungs.

Allegra smelled of annoyance and ... conspiracy? Deception? The pink-purple, fragrant lily scent of deception tangled around the dusty mustard color of her annoyance, but you didn't need a Scenter to see how irritated she was.

"And how does he expect me to house five more drifters?" Her mouth was tight.

"Drifters?" Anglarok's face went red, his emotions escalating suddenly to scarlet fury. "You address the Ki'squall of the Harbingers, merchant, and you will pay for your insolence!"

"Wait!" Marielle yelled, leaping to get between the two of them. She felt ill at the memory of a head falling heavy off the lifeless body of the man in the District above. These people would slay Allegra without thinking. "Stop! There will be no paying for anything right now. By the authority of the Jingen City Watch, you will halt this disruption of the peace under Article V section 34, which states that no citizen may cause or threaten to cause bodily harm over an insult or perceived insult but must take their case to the arbiter for a decision."

Allegra was looking at her wide-eyed like she'd grown a second head, surprise in raspberry clouds mixed with a sudden burst of pineapple insight.

"I'll find a place for you all in the back while we wait for Etienne or until I can find an alternative situation," she said, carefully. "We've finished cleaning there. I have no food, I'm afraid, not during the fast, but there is green tea."

There was a long moment as Marielle held her breath. Liandari glanced at Anglarok who gave a quick nod before she looked back at Allegra.

"We will tolerate that. For now."

Marielle felt a stab of fear at the injured pride on both sides, washing off of them in waves of indigo blue. This was not going to end well.

"And I'll add the cost to what you owe me," Allegra said to Marielle through gritted teeth. And there it was. The threat that she knew was coming.

"Is Tamerlan awake yet?" she asked.

"Awake and long gone," Allegra said, as she led them into the back.

Marielle froze, hesitating for a moment.

Gone? He was already gone? She needed to find him! He shouldn't be wandering out there on his own. She had questions for him. She'd fought to keep him alive and now he was just … gone. Didn't he owe her more than that?

But he didn't, did he? He'd saved her life. She'd saved his. They were even. Except for this price that Allegra planned to exact from her.

A hand rested on her arm. She looked up to see Anglarok's face looking down at her over his scarf. He pulled the scarf down before he spoke and she did the same, trying not to be bowled over by the pungent scent of Allegra's wares.

"You aren't planning to go back out there again, are you? You could smell that crowd. It is not safe for Windsniffers outside right now. That hunt has them on edge. They see us only as bloodhounds. Stay here with us and drink tea. I have a gift for you that will be worth whatever price this daughter of a shark is demanding of you."

He smiled a fierce but magical smile and Marielle couldn't help but smile too, despite the shiver in her bones. Jhinn had said not to accept any gifts. But she had a creeping suspicion that Anglarok and the others wouldn't take 'no' without insult.

They found a place between bales of spices. A small table and chairs were set up there, and bales of sweet-smelling grasses were set around the edges – comfortable places to sit or lay items on. Around them, bales of spice rose to the rafters and clumps of dried herbs hung in bunches as big as Marielle, drying in the warehouse. The bales dampened sound and it felt as if they were cut off from the outside world as Allegra settled them in.

"Tea will be here momentarily," she said through clenched teeth. "I will return to be sure that you have what you need. And now, if I may borrow Marielle for a moment."

She seized Marielle's arm in her vice-like grip and with a smile for the Harbingers – as false as the fragrant lily smell attached to it, she marched Marielle out of the room made of bales and into a small side room where citrus peel had been carefully sliced and was left on the table half-threaded onto drying lines.

"Did Etienne say why he is helping these foreigners?" she hissed.

"They come from the sails in the distance," Marielle said. "They are forerunners of that invasion – or whatever it is."

"Dragon's spit in a cup! He'll ruin everything. He said no more?"

"He didn't say anything," Marielle said.

"Dragon's blood and ashes!" Fury poured off her in red waves and Marielle coughed, choking on the sudden smell pitch. "Well, I was planning to keep you waiting, but it seems my hand is tipped. It's time to collect payment."

Marielle felt her spine freeze as she watched Allegra chew at her lip and stare at Marielle. She smelled of uncertainty and worry. Garlic and smoked paprika ringed her, swirling in ribbons of ochre and heather.

"I don't like trusting people." And that made sense since she didn't smell of truth or trust. "And I hate to trust you, but you owe me a debt and you must pay it, yes?"

"Yes," Marielle agreed, though the word was bitter on her tongue.

"So, this is how you will pay. You will watch Etienne for me and report on what he is doing, who he is speaking to, and what plans he is making. Keep your eyes open and that nose of yours glued to the trail. I know he will keep you close – for your blood and skills if nothing else. And you must serve him. Because you owe him something – I don't know what and I don't need to know – but I know enough to know you can't slip loose. So, if you're to be by his side, best that you are there as my cat's paw. Remember: watch, report, stay close."

Marielle's mouth twisted at the demand. She was a servant of the law, not a spy. She was looking for redemption, not complications. She wanted to serve, not to scheme.

"You owe me. And the law demands that you pay according to my terms," Allegra said, lifting an eyebrow.

And she was right. The law did demand that Marielle pay her debt. Any arbiter would rule that way.

"You agree?" Allegra prodded.

"I agree," Marielle said, and she felt like a traitor for saying it.

# 13: A Strange Pairing

"You think the Eye is here?" Lord Mythos asked quietly as they stood side by side regarding the mausoleum of King Abelmeyer.

Tamerlan gasped for breath. The journey – even just to the Alchemist District – had been hard on his shoulder and his vision was blacking in and out as he fought to catch his breath.

"Drink," Lord Mythos said, shoving a small flask into his hands.

Thankfully, it was water. A small sip and he was already recovering a little, his breath coming a little easier, his vision clearing.

"Why bury a king in the Alchemist's District?"

"It wasn't the Alchemist District when he was buried," Mythos said, circling the tall spire. Made of white stone and chiseled into a perfect point, it rose high in the middle of the Alchemist's District of Xin. Amidst the colorful plumes of smoke pouring from the windows of a nearby Alchemy House – *The Brass Cauldron* – the pale spire looked strange. The simple stone box beneath it – as tall as Tamerlan and just as wide – was just as strange. There was no inscription. No plaque. No flowers. Nothing except chipped cobblestones and a smell that suggested it was being used as an alternative lavatory.

Around them, the sounds and smells of the busy Alchemist District filled Tamerlan with a strange feeling of nostalgia. Strange because he'd hated his life as an alchemist. Strange, because he felt nothing but guilt at the memories of those lost. Stranger still because he almost felt an itch to grind up ingredients, chopping, weighing, drying, compounding ...

*And then open the Bridge and call us forth!*

He clamped down on his own thoughts. That pathway led to danger.

"How did my sister escape Jingen?" he asked. "She was right in the heart of the city."

*You'll be sorry that you didn't call ...*

"A lot of Landholds in Jingen were in the Seven Suns Palace," Lord Mythos said as he walked around the mausoleum, feeling the stone with his hands. "They knew about the *Lady Luck* – a small ship tucked away in the Government District. It's possible that is how she escaped. Possible that they rode the canal down to the river – just like you did. Just like most of the survivors from the heart of the city did. I don't know for sure, but if I was a betting man, that's what I'd bet on. Everyone else was crushed, trampled, drowned, or fell from a great height.

Do you want me to go on? Do you want me to help you revel in what you did?"

"If I hadn't done it, you would have slit Marielle's throat and drained her blood to appease your dragon," he said bitterly. Because what he'd done hadn't been all bad. He'd only ever wanted to save the innocent. His face felt hot at the thought because for all his good wishes, he'd only achieved evil. Except for her. Except for Marielle. "And why are you feeling the stones? If I was hiding something valuable in a tomb, I wouldn't put it in a loose stone, I would put it in one of the drawers under the corpse. You know, the locked ones for valuables."

Lord Mythos' eyebrows rose. "How do you know about what lies inside a mausoleum?"

"I read," Tamerlan said simply, showing him the book they'd stolen when they crept out of the Library. On the page was a diagram of the mausoleum. And the drawers were clearly marked. "There's even a list of valuables. But there's no mention of an amulet. Maybe it's in the barrow."

"Hmmm," Lord Mythos said, laying his hand over the lock on the mausoleum. He closed his eyes. "There is no barrow. That is just legend. And I did not wish to kill Marielle. But look at the alternative. Thousands dead and left to rot unburied. Children. Babies. People's parents and lovers and children. Tell me honestly that knowing what you know now, you'd choose to save her again." Tamerlan swallowed and with his eyes still closed, Lord Mythos snorted. "See? You wouldn't have stopped me if you knew. I don't know why people ignore the catechism. It's so clear."

"Because it's just old dusty words. Tradition. Legend. Things that couldn't possibly be real. No one really thinks those things still have power."

"And yet they do. They're all real. And they are all deadly."

Tamerlan shivered.

"And if we don't stop this dragon, he will kill again. Sure, the other cities completed their rituals. The other Lady Sacrifices died. But that won't save them when Jingen returns."

"Returns? You're planning to restore the city?"

Lord Mythos laughed. "The cities, Tamerlan, were named for the dragons. The dragon is also named Jingen, just like the dragon sleeping under this city is named Xin – have you forgotten that? And I am about to borrow a tiny ficker of what belongs to Xin."

A click in the lock punctuated his words and the door to the mausoleum swung open.

"You'd think that there would be guards," Tamerlan said, looking around. People passed by on every side, going about their business. No one seemed to have noticed that the mausoleum door was open a crack.

"You don't need to guard things lying in plain sight. Almost everyone ignores their significance. Watch my back." He ducked into the mausoleum so quickly that Tamerlan swallowed in surprise, his eyes opening wide as he closed the door carefully behind Lord Mythos. He'd rather not get in trouble with the City Watch in *two* cities.

His mouth was dry as he kept watch. Even though he'd lost the cloak, his armor still stood out in this district. There weren't many alchemists wandering around in full guard's kit carrying bastard swords. But the people here seemed to almost instinctually look away from a man in armor. He probably would have, too. In Jingen, officers only meant trouble.

He tried to concentrate on keeping watch, but it was hard to keep his eyes on the city when they kept flicking back to the book in his hands.

*The mausoleum is said to be a focal point for the energy of Xin, a place where magic can be harnessed by the right kind of mind. A place of focus. Perhaps it is the bones of King Abelmeyer that made it so. It is said that he laid a curse on them, that the day the dragon Xin rises again, King Abelmeyer will rise, too, and walk the world in his own bones. He will be a scourge to those who have forgotten the traditions and the recompense for their many sins.*

He glanced up to see someone standing in the street watching him. Ooops.

He knocked on the door to the mausoleum. Hopefully, Lord Mythos would hear and come out. Right now, he was beginning to draw eyes. Someone else stopped, pointing at him. He flipped a page, trying to look casual.

There was a picture of King Abelmeyer being buried. Someone had taken time to sketch him in his final resting place, the amulet lying on his chest.

So, it really was here at one time.

He heard a scraping sound behind him, but he didn't glance back. He was large and tall. Perhaps Lord Mythos could slip out of the mausoleum and no one would see him behind Tamerlan's broad shoulders. The men on the street were growing into a knot of murmuring spectators. That wasn't good.

"Mythos?" He said quietly.

"Call me Etienne."

"I think we should be going now, Etienne." Standing still had made his chest seize up and now he could barely move his arm as he tried to adjust the book.

"The tomb was empty."

"No amulet?" He asked as Lord Mythos slipped in front of him, also trying to appear casual.

"Completely empty. There weren't even bones."

Tamerlan felt the blood draining from his face. That couldn't be good. Had King Abelmeyer's bones already risen from the dead? And was he really thinking superstitious thoughts like that?

"You need more water," Etienne said, pulling his flash from his pocket again. It must have caught the light. That was the only explanation for why one of the men in the knot lunged forward.

"They've found something!" he called.

"Nothing at all!" Etienne said with raised hands, but it didn't matter.

Already, people were surging forward from every direction.

"Think you can run?" Etienne asked, pulled the library book from Tamerlan's hands.

"No."

"Too bad. You're going to have to. See if you can use some of that magic you stole in Jingen."

"I didn't steal magic!" Tamerlan protested, but the Lord Mythos was already running, a dark streak in the colorful crowds and with a groan, Tamerlan followed, every jarring step its own small agony.

He was going to die chasing after a man who hated him. He felt heat as fresh blood washed down from his shoulder, soaking his bandage and then his clothing, hot and wet and flaring with pain with every step he took. His head was light, his vision crackling around the edges.

They reached a canal and he heard Etienne yelling to the gondolier – was there something familiar about that gondolier? – but he could hardly think, hardly even make his pounding heart slow down long enough to listen.

He stumbled forward, his vision darkening. Rough hands tossed him into the boat and then he was huddled in the bottom of the gondola as it shot down the canal and Etienne continued to scold the gondolier.

"I'm telling you, I'll pay you, just get us out of here." Frustration dripped from his tone. "Stay with me, Tamerlan!"

There was a crash in the distance and Tamerlan heard Etienne calling something to his pursuers, but he didn't make out the words. Pain pulled him into a hot embrace and blackness quickly followed, swallowing him up.

# 14: Wind Rose

*MARIELLE*

It turned out that Allegra owned the inn next door. It also turned out that she grew impatient quickly and when Etienne took longer than expected, she opened a secret door from her warehouse to the inn and moved the Harbingers there.

"But don't expect me to do this for nothing," she told them. "You owe me now."

"How much?" Liandari had asked with a curl of her lip. "What is your price, shopkeeper?"

Allegra's lips had tightened then but her expression turned to one of shock when Lindari flicked a finger against her thumb and one of her silent harpooners pulled three pearls the size of large peas from a small leather bag and handed them to Allegra.

"For a week. Food included," Liandari said. Allegra opened her mouth and the Ki'squall bared her teeth with a puff of garnet and pitch fury. "Try to negotiate and we will spear you where you stand."

Allegra's mouth shut with a click and she escorted them through the hidden door and up to a suite of rooms in the top floor of the inn.

"Send refreshment up. I grow weary of this city," Liandari had said and though Allegra's mouth tightened, and her scent was filled with sulfur and lime scented agitation, swirling around her in dusty clouds, still she left without a word.

Satisfaction surrounded the Ki'squall in bright apricot hues. And no wonder. She'd been left to cool her heels in a storage warehouse instead of being shown here right away. Would Allegra have treated a Landhold that way? Why was she so eager to push these people around when Lord Mythos wanted them for allies?

"Why did you come to the Dragonblood Plains?" Marielle asked as the Ki'squall settled in a padded ottoman, looking out over the city from a wide balcony where filmy curtains hid her from view while still allowing her to see everything beyond. "Was it only that prophecy?"

"One of the dragons has risen into the sky," she said, her voice tired. "And for that crime, Queen Mer will demand retribution."

Marielle shivered.

"The Bridge of Legends has been opened once more," the Windsniffer said, casting an unreadable glance toward Liandari and then pouring water from a jug at the central table.

The harpooners had settled in without a word – two guarding the door, two taking to their rooms in the suite immediately.

They worked in silence. Marielle was beginning to wonder if they could speak at all.

"And this time," he said, moving to the wide window to look out, too, "there are new Legends. New problems."

"What is the Bridge of Legends?" Marielle asked.

"A path from one world to another. From the land where the heroes and villains wait to rise once more – to our world."

"Like the Legends from the stories? King Abelmeyer? Lady Chaos? Queen Mer?"

They glanced at each other and it worried Marielle that they smelled of silver truth and certainty. It worried her more that this sounded so familiar. What had Tamerlan done, after all, but access these Legends – if Jhinn were to be believed?

"Those are the new Legends. Before they rose to take that place, there were other legends. Darker Legends. The Legends that commanded the dragons ... and other creatures."

Marielle shivered. "Other creatures?"

"There were many dark evils fighting man for this world in the days of the former Legends. And then men found a way to take the Legends and use them for their own purposes. It was a dark time. A time of chaos and deep evil."

"Why doesn't anyone talk about that?"

He shrugged. "Maybe it's easier to forget. Maybe it's simpler. But the People of Queen Mer's Retribution do not forget. And we have returned to teach your people and remind them again of what they have forgotten."

"Then why are you the only ones who have come from the ships?" Marielle asked. She felt Liandari stiffen at her question, but Anglarok merely smiled.

"You can't go outside right now." They'd heard a rumor as they were taken upstairs. Things were worse in the city. Mobs were forming. Scenters being snatched off the streets. What they had seen had only been the beginning. "So, it seems that now would be a good time to begin your lessons, hmmm? I'm surprised you are so untrained. Even in this backward land."

"Untrained?" Marielle almost laughed. "I spent my youth in the Scenter Academy, learning to hone my senses and being educated in the ways of the world, the laws of Jingen, the catechisms of the Dragonblood Plains and our traditions."

He waved a hand as if that mattered little, his scent – sea salt and strange spices she couldn't identify mixed with the silver and mint of certainty – was steady and unruffled. "But no magic, it would seem."

"Magic?" Awe filled her voice and a tiny thrill of anticipation. She could almost taste the lilac and vanilla of magic on her tongue at the very thought of it.

His eyes were bright and a smile began to form on his oak-hard face. "Sit with me."

They sat in a pair of upholstered chairs a little off to the side from the ottoman where Liandari continued to observe the city below.

Anglarok ran a hand through dark hair, "There are many kinds of magic in this world. Our gift – the gift of scent – is not magic at all, but rather just a heightening of the senses. It can be refined and encouraged. It can also be augmented and for that, we can use magic."

Marielle licked her lips and Anglarok tilted his head like he was smelling something coming from her.

"But now I see that I have made you overeager," he said, an agitated look flooding his face as he bit his lip, watching her. "It is a long time since I have been a Wind Guide. The balance of this is delicate."

He wiped his brow and then tore off his coat and the light shirt beneath it, revealing a chest and arms as tattooed as the harpooners'. Small trails went up the edges of his neck and as far as his hands, wrapping around his body in whorls just a little darker than his already dark skin.

They really were maps! She could see coastlines picked out in careful detail and small islands, towns and cities, mountains, eddies, and whorls in the sea. Each named. There were coordinates beside some. And over his heart was a starburst inside a circle. The points of the starburst reached past the circle. Small, but significant and located on an isle in the sea.

He tapped on his heart. "These tattoos show where I have been and where I am from. Starting here, at my home island. I add to these as I travel, recording the places I have been and the things I have seen on my skin – a memory stamped forever on my body. Magic is like that. It leaves a mark. Every bit of it you touch will change you. Which is why you need more caution. You need more care before you can touch it. Because the unwary can be quickly consumed, burned up by the power of the unknown and the fires they start can burn the world."

Marielle shivered. They'd woken the dragon by playing with magic. And the world was already beginning to burn.

"But can't you do good with magic, too?"

He nodded. "But magic is used much more often for evil than for good. And even the good we cause can accidentally do evil, too. Power is always dangerous. The more of it that there is, the more dangerous it becomes. Long, long ago, Queen Mer rode the waves, dispensing justice and mercy at her will." He tapped on an eddy in the waters on his ribcage. "And in this place, she waits, ready to return, ready to judge. We feel her waking from her slumber. We must be ready."

"And that's why you are here," Marielle nodded.

"The dragons are rising. The Dragonblooded have broken their vows. If the world is in chaos when the Queen returns, she will bring judgment on us all," his words were quiet but grim. "We must restore order. We must close the Bridge of Legends. We must find the key. We must lock up the dragons again."

"I want that, too," Marielle said. "I want to restore order. I want good laws and justice."

He smiled, cider-scented contentment rolling off him like heat waves. "Then don't be too eager to leap into magic, Marielle."

"Enough," Liandari said from her seat on the ottoman. "If you plan to fold her into our ranks, Anglarok, then have her accept the Wind Rose. If she does not agree, then she knows too much already."

"The Wind Rose?" Marielle asked.

He tapped his chest where the starburst and circle sat. "This. The sign that you are pledged to Queen Mer and the sea."

"What does that mean?" Marielle asked nervously. For Jhinn, it meant never leaving the sea. For these people, it seemed to mean vengeance, but also order. She wasn't sure she wanted that.

She had expected Anglarok to answer, but it was Liandari who spoke, "You will take the vow of our ancestors, '*Seas send as you may, wind blow as you may, I am but a ship on the waters. I am but a vessel of justice and righteousness. Though many waters roll below me, though waves crash all around, still I am whole on the peak of chaos, still I climb to the top of the spray.*'"

Marielle shivered.

"It's a pledge of justice and righteousness and a promise not to let chaos sink you. There is more to it, more to learn from us Windsniffers – but that is all you pledge to begin. It's a solemn vow. You can't turn away from it once you begin. It will set your compass and guide your path."

"But who wouldn't want to promise to be just and righteous?" Marielle asked. "Who wouldn't be willing to promise to keep trying?"

Liandari snorted derisively. "Lazy oafs. The twisted. Anyone who is not woven of moral fiber. Weak ropes and rotten docks, all of them."

Anglarok cleared his throat and she blushed, looking back out the balcony window, her eyes glued to the white sail in the distance.

"I grow weary of waiting," she declared. "I will rest until this Etienne Velendark returns or until morning, whichever comes first. Then we will act."

She strode to one of the bedrooms and shut the door behind her.

"And you, Marielle?" Anglarok asked. "Will you take the Wind Rose?"

Jhinn had warned her not to accept gifts from the Harbingers, but he was only a boy. What could he know about this? If the Jingen City Watch still existed, that would be different. She could keep protecting the people and keeping the law, but it didn't exist anymore, and it wouldn't exist again unless they brought down the dragon.

"I've promised to help Etienne stop the dragon. I've promised to guard him," she said, hesitating.

"And you think a pledge to do what is right would interfere with that?" his words were silky smooth, but he smelled only of determination – peppermint and crisp blue. He was serious about this. And he wasn't trying to trick her.

She wet her lips with her tongue. Order sang to her like a distant siren. Her laws were gone, washed away with the emerging dragon, but she could uphold new laws – laws baked into a culture so dedicated to them that they made each member swear to live a life of justice. It was hard not to feel giddy at the thought of that, but she had to be certain before she made any kind of pledge.

"And that's all that will be required of me – only what is said in that vow?"

"Of course." There had to be a catch, didn't there? And yet Anglarok's expression was open and honest and he smelled of silver and mint truth with only the barest hint of lavender. What could possibly be wrong about that? "Join us in upholding the law, Marielle. Join us in pursuing evil and destroying it. Let us give you tools beyond what you could imagine to conquer this evil in your land. And pledge to pursue justice and righteousness with us."

She was nodding before he had even finished already wanting it so badly that she felt she could taste justice on the tip of her tongue and purpose in the scent she breathed in.

"I want what you have," she said, feeling almost giddy as she made her decision. She never even noticed the vanilla and lilac tinting the air so slightly that it was hardly discernable at all.

# 15: BLACK AND WHITE

*MARIELLE*

Marielle's teeth were on edge when she finally returned to *Spellspinner's Cures*. The Wind Rose on the upper part of her chest burned and since getting it, she felt both lightheaded and as if she really was riding a wave of passion and certainty. It felt so good to have a driving force behind her again. She was like a sail in need of a wind, like a gondola in need of the water. And it felt so right to have the wind at her back again and the tide under her feet.

Allegra was closing her shop when Marielle returned. She lifted her eyebrows as Marielle stepped into the main shop as Allegra was pinching out the candles in the window.

"You seem to enjoy the company of our guests," she said mildly.

"Etienne asked me to watch them." Allegra was hard to talk to without sounding stilted. You could feel hostility radiating from her like a stove. And yet that was not what she smelled of. She smelled of passion and secrecy, a strange mix of birch

123

smoke and fragrant lilies, swirling around her in reds and pinkish purples. She glowed so brightly from her powerful emotions that she outshone the candles.

There were other smells in *Spellspinner's Cures* laid out over the powerful scents of the spices in the back, and Marielle could smell the comings and goings of the day. Customers with worries lacing their steps, ambitions swirling in their movements, anxiety frizzling off them and leaving residues across everything they touched. And something else. Deceit swirled in the air in greenish-yellow, smelling of caramel. Something was going on a *Spellspinner's Cures* – some plan that Marielle knew nothing about.

"He's not back yet." Worry puffed around her in ochre clouds, but before Marielle could respond, a rap sounded at the door.

Allegra, already nearby, lifted the bar and the door burst open.

Etienne stumbled into Spellspinner's Cures, carrying a dazed Tamerlan in his arms.

"He lost consciousness when we hit the Spice District," he said with a gasp as Marielle rushed forward to help. "The city has gone mad. Lady Saga doomed us all with this hunt. Here, help me."

"That's not the only way," Allegra said with an angry twist to her mouth but there wasn't time for Marielle to wonder at the puff of mushroom scent surrounding her.

Etienne stumbled as he tried to hold onto the bigger man. It was amazing that he'd carried Tamerlan as far as he had. Etienne was short and compact, and while his slender frame was strong, he was more than a head shorter than Tamerlan and not nearly as thick in the shoulders.

Marielle slipped an arm under Tamerlan's, letting his head loll onto her shoulder. A dark patch spread across his shirt and he was missing his blue cloak.

Allegra clucked her tongue, taking the other side of him.

"How are we going to get him up the stairs?" Marielle asked.

"Just let me catch my breath a moment," Etienne said, leaning against the barred door as he sucked in huge breaths. Marielle watched him, mesmerized by his youth. He carried so much weight on him – so many plots and hopes and tragedies – for such a young man. And he never smelled of anxiety, only certainty and truth, swirling mint and sliver and intermingling with the royal blue and gardenia power and his own scent – tangerines and cloves. He was a puzzle. And she wanted to figure him out.

But not right now. Right now, they needed to help Tamerlan.

"What were you doing together?" she asked him.

"Hunting the Eye. We'll need it to tame the dragon. To bind him once more."

She shivered. That was all she wanted, too. It was why she shied away from Tamerlan's slumped body every time it brushed against the burning skin of her upper chest where the Wind Rose had been tattooed only an hour ago.

"Everyone will want the Eye," Allegra said coolly, "for good or ill."

She smelled of ambition – roasting meat and russet swirls. She wanted the amulet, too. And the way her cold eyes were turned on Etienne, Marielle thought that perhaps if he found it, that would be the payment she would exact for all her generosity. Just watching that hawk-eyed glance made Marielle's hackles rise.

"Yes, they do," Etienne said, taking Allegra's place under Tamerlan's arm. "You take his feet." As she scrambled to pick them up, he continued. "I watched a Scenter ripped apart in the street – Xin City Watch – two groups wanted her. Neither would back down, not even when her screams shattered the air and then stilled as they clawed through the rags of her clothing."

Marielle felt light-headed as they climbed the stairs. What would have happened to her if Liandari hadn't stepped in?

After a moment, Etienne added, "You need to stay out of sight, Marielle. You need to stay here while this hunt continues. You understand?"

Marielle nodded as they crested the last stair and hurried to Tamerlan's bedroom. "I will."

"I need to see to Queen Mer's people," Etienne said after they laid Tamerlan on the bed. He looked bone weary.

"And I want to speak to you about them," Allegra said, her eyes narrowing and her scent smelling of jasmine concentration. She turned to Marielle, pointing to a small fireplace in the room. "Strip him to his small clothes and boil

126

water. I'll be back to clean and dress the wound. Fool man. He should have returned hours ago."

"We were mired in the crowds," Etienne explained as they left together.

Marielle clenched her jaw. She wanted to hear what else they had to say. If she was going to be stuck in these buildings for the next few days, she itched to know why. More than that, she wanted to hear what Etienne would say to the Harbingers. Especially now that she was linked to them.

With a sigh, she lit a fire, scooping water from a barrel next to it into a kettle and setting it on the hook above the flames. The fire lit easily, and she moved to Tamerlan.

He moaned as she tugged off his boots. They were wet and muddy. She threw them to the side by the wall and worked to unbuckle his belt and remove his sword. As she slid the belt off, his eyes flickered open.

"Marielle," he sounded feverish.

"Shhh," she said, gently pulling the belt free and hanging it on the hooks by the door. The sword was heavy, dragging at the belt. "You're safe here, Tamerlan."

He looked around, his eyes glassy, still muttering feverishly. "Trying to help the Lord Mythos find the Eye."

"Yes, I know," she said, tugging at his light armor. How did it come off? Ah! She found the leather straps, the tip of her tongue sticking out as she concentrated to loosen them.

"Trying to make it all right. Dragon." His face was slick with sweat. It highlighted the stubble along his jaw and the sharp lines of his face.

She paused, looking at him, compassion and frustration warring inside her. He wanted to make it all right again? He wanted what she wanted.

And she was torn because part of her wanted to appreciate that desire and part of her thought it was unfair that he might find redemption when she still hadn't found it. After all, she wouldn't be in this mess without him.

"Are you sorry that you rescued me?" she asked gently as she pulled the armor off, piece by piece, and set it to the side of the bed.

"All those people. Innocent people." His breathing was labored as he rambled. "Dragon. I killed them."

The fever must be bad for him to be mumbling 'dragon' every few minutes. Marielle flinched from the thought of the dragon. He haunted them both. And he would destroy everything if he wasn't stopped. But running all over the city looking for a lost amulet didn't sound like the right way to stop him. The Harbingers had magic of their own. That would be a better way to stop a dragon.

"Marielle?" his voice, faint but still resonant as it had been the first time she met him, twisted with the golden scent of her attraction to him. It rose up with his own scent, making her mouth water with the cinnamon and honey scent of him. She was as drawn to it as ever, despite every reason she had not to be.

"Yes?" she asked as she gently tugged his tabard up and over his head, flinching when pain flashed across his face.

"Can you ever forgive me?" the words dropped from his mouth heavy and full of pain and with them, the golden attraction she felt for him flooded the room so strongly that it was more powerful to her than the turquoise and lilac of magic. More powerful than the guilt she felt over what her life had cost the world. It made her want to say 'yes' just to soothe him, just to make him smile.

"I don't know," she said, softly, honestly.

"I hope that you can someday." His words were faint, and his eyes drooped.

She chewed her lip, closing her own eyes for a moment as pain swept over her. She was as much at fault as he was. Everything he'd done, she'd been complicit in. But how could you forgive something so horrific? How could anyone ever atone for that?

He was wicked and beautiful, tainted and attractive. He was utterly out of reach.

She cleared her throat, gently tugging the tabard over his head as he hissed in pain. It would need to be cleaned. It was soaked in blood. She hung it on one of the hooks and began to pull his shirt out of his breeches, tugging it free gently. She could feel her cheeks heating up. Practically, he needed to be undressed for his wounds to be tended. But she'd never undressed a man before and it felt – invasive. Like she shouldn't be doing it. Like it was a small kind of crime.

He flinched from the pain with every tug of his clothing.

"Marielle?" he asked, his voice soft and thick.

"Yes?" she asked as she gently worked his shirt over his right arm and then peeled it bit by bit from the drying blood on his chest. His body was hard and strong under the bloody shirt. He could recover from this – she was sure of it.

"What do the laws say about forgiveness. Is it even possible? For someone like me?"

They said it wasn't. They said he should sink. They said there was no redemption for a person like Tamerlan.

But why not?

He lay there, his face smooth in his half-conscious state, his big, calloused hands lying still and vulnerable on the narrow bed. It was his eyelashes that made him look the most innocent. They lay on his cheek like a child's and she traced their soft edges with her gaze, letting it wander over his slightly parted lips and his blood-crusted chest as it rose and fell. He looked so innocent. He looked so young.

And he wasn't innocent at all anymore. Did it matter that he'd done it all to save someone else? It mattered to him. It wouldn't matter to the desperate survivors, mourning lost friends. It wouldn't matter to the dead.

And yet … couldn't there be some hope for a man like this? What would Captain Ironarm have thought? She'd said it was moments like this where a Watch Officer really knew what she was made of. What had she meant by that? Had she meant that Marielle should be iron hard, not letting emotions or sympathy get in the way? Or had she meant that Marielle would see that not everything was so easy to judge? Some things were murkier than she could imagine.

She felt the Wind Rose over her heart – a renewed commitment to justice. She just wasn't sure. Everything was so tangled that she lost sight of one end of the thread by the time she got to the other end.

"I don't think there *is* forgiveness for someone like you, Tamerlan," she said thickly as she slid his shirt over his head. She was sad to be the one to say this. But wasn't honesty better than lies? Didn't she at least owe him that? "Not for the butcher of the Temple District. Not for the man who destroyed thousands of lives."

He shuddered as the shirt came free, his eyes opening groggily. "Be careful, Marielle. With words like that, you might make me fall in love with you."

Was that a joke? She licked her lips. It had sounded a little bit too real.

His eyes closed again but he grunted when she spread the sheet over his battered body – she left his dirty breeches on him. She wouldn't invade his privacy enough to remove them. If Allegra didn't like that – well, Allegra didn't seem to like much of anything.

His chest wound was open and bleeding, the blood crusting at the edges now that he was lying still in the bed. Just looking at it made her flinch.

The water in the kettle was boiling. In a moment, Allegra would return, and she would patch him up again, but right now he was suffering for his sins, one breath at a time, and Marielle wasn't even sure if she thought that was a good thing or a terrible one – just or unjust.

She sighed, wishing that the world was as black and white as her vision was. If only things were simpler. If only he didn't smell like life and hope when he was nothing but death and despair.

# DAWNING

# SECOND DAY
## OF
# DAWNSPELL

# 16: TENACITY'S PLAYTHING

*TAMERLAN*

Tamerlan woke to a snore. Surprisingly, it was Marielle. It looked like she'd been sitting in a chair beside the foot of his bed and had fallen asleep and slumped over the foot of the bed.

Had he really asked her for forgiveness last night?

And had she really denied him?

That part made sense. He wasn't sure that there was anyone who could ever absolve him for what he'd done. Not sure that he'd want to meet a person who would. What kind of crimes would a person have had to have committed to be able to shrug at Tamerlan's?

And yet, that was all he wanted. It burned in him like a flame. He was going to find a way to redeem himself or die trying.

Marielle's shirt parted where she was slumped across the foot of the bed, showing the upper part of her chest where someone had tattooed a many-pointed star recently. It reminded him of a compass. Fitting. After all, she was like a moral compass, always pointing due-justice. He smiled as he watched her sleep, her snores filling the tiny room. She was too beautiful for that guard's uniform. Too beautiful for the rough cloth and leather that she dressed in. Her long black hair had untangled from its braid and it wrapped around her like black ribbons. He felt a smile start to form but it slipped from his face when he tried to sit up.

He bit back a moan. Someone had dressed and cared for his wound, but it hurt more now than it had yesterday. Bruising spread across his chest, black and splotchy. Everything hurt. And he was mostly naked. How had that happened? He felt his cheeks heating at the memory of a small pair of hands undressing him.

Carefully, he pulled his feet from the bedclothes, trying not to disturb Marielle. She seemed unhurt beyond the tattoo – and they were safe here. At least there was that.

His clothes hung from hooks, bloodstained and muddy. They were going to be awkward to dress in.

He flinched as the door opened and Etienne walked in. He took one look at Marielle spread across the end of the bed, her legs still on the stool beside the bed and one look at Tamerlan frozen as he was about to stand. His eyebrow rose and he shook his head, his eyes narrowing for a moment as they caught on Marielle's tattoo.

He threw a bundle of cloth at Tamerlan, speaking quietly. "Today we'll dress down and blend in. Leave the armor. Bring the sword."

Tamerlan nodded, grateful when the door closed behind the Lord Mythos and he could dress as slowly and painfully as he needed. The clothing was simple – tradesmen's clothes. He was used to those. Even so, it was long minutes before he was dressed and pulling his sword belt on.

He leaned down as he was leaving, laying a palm for a moment on Marielle's sleeping head. She hated him. She could never forgive him. And yet, she'd sat here all night guarding him while he thrashed from nightmares and memories. What kind of golden heart cared for an enemy like that? She deserved the very best.

"Ready?" Etienne asked the moment he stepped out of the room.

Tamerlan nodded. He felt anything but ready. What he needed was rest and time to heal. What he wanted was to stop this dragon before it was too late to ever find his soul again.

*Dragon.*

Any mention of a dragon set Ram off again. He'd muttered to Tamerlan all night, an endless litany of obsession. No wonder no one spoke of him. If he was as obsessive in life as he was in his afterlife, he couldn't have had many friends.

*Dragon. Dragon. Dragon.*

Etienne coughed. "I had to carry you back here last night."

Tamerlan felt his cheeks heat at the thought. Now he owed the Lord Mythos another debt he couldn't repay.

"Thank you."

"I can't take Marielle with me. The city is ripping Scenters to pieces," he said, shifting his weight uncomfortably, like he had something on his mind.

Tamerlan adjusted his sword. It would be hard to wield with his wound, but he would do as he must.

"So, I need you," Etienne continued, clearly torn. After a moment he sighed and laid a hand on Tamerlan's injured shoulder. Tamerlan flinched from the touch, but before he could even gasp in pain, fire scorched his flesh, followed by ice ripping through his body. He gasped, thinking he was dying as he collapsed to one knee, clutching at the wall for support. Everything hurt. Everything ached.

*He's killing you! Fight back!* He didn't even know which Legend was screaming in his mind, but he agreed. He was going to die.

And then, quick as a heartbeat, the pain was gone completely, leaving him sucking in deep lungfuls of air.

"You still have magic," he gasped. "Why didn't you use that before?"

"I'd hoped to avoid it. It's not mine to use."

*Magic belongs to no one but the one who takes it.* Tamerlan wasn't sure if that was his thought or one of the Legends. They were beginning to sound too familiar in his mind so that sometimes their thoughts felt like his. Did that mean he was going crazy?

He worked his shoulder experimentally. It felt fine, the muscles moving easily. He drew in a breath – the first one in a long time that came easily.

"Why do that for *me?*"

His belly rumbled loudly, reminding him that he hadn't eaten in days. Etienne shoved a water flask toward him, and he drank deeply as the other man spoke before climbing back to his feet.

"It's Dawning – no food anywhere in the city. You could use some, but you'll have to go without. Call it your part of the payment for the magic I stole."

"How does hunger pay for anything?" Tamerlan asked.

Etienne gave him a burning look. "Suffering is a form of payment. You'll find that out. Everyone does eventually. We all pay for what we want in time, energy, or health. Today, you pay in health. Now, come on. No time to waste. I have an idea of where we can look for the Eye."

Etienne's idea was a bridge. *Dragon Collar Bridge,* to be exact.

Which was how Tamerlan found himself in the rising dawn, looking over the side of the tallest bridge he'd ever seen. It spanned between the Library District of Xin and the outer wall of the city, rising up, up, up into the air. A canal and a set of locks worked under the bridge, and even in the early morning, it was packed with boats.

Tamerlan felt a thrill of something close to apprehension. It left gooseflesh over his whole body. The last time he'd looked at a bridge it had been flying right for him as the dragon Jingen flicked his tail. He gritted his teeth. That wasn't going to happen today.

He scanned the sky looking for a dragon silhouette. Well, it might not happen today. If they were lucky. That dragon would return sometime. It had to.

He shook himself back to reality.

It made sense to check this bridge. It was built during the time of King Abelmeyer. And it was rumored to have a hidden room in the footings, though right now Lord Mythos was striding along the bridge, inspecting the rails.

*The amulet is not in the bridge,* Lila Cherrylocks told him boldly.

Tamerlan tried to shove her from his mind. The more he listened to the Legends, the more they felt real. But they weren't real, were they? Not if he didn't smoke.

*Oh, you'll smoke again. You can't stop now. Not when you have access to all of this.*

She didn't know him.

From the *Dragon Collar Bridge,* he could see the smoke still rising from the ruins of Jingen. Never again.

*You'll have to. If you want to find this amulet. Only one of us can tell you where it is.*

A ruse. To trick him into evil. Lila was a trickster and he should never forget it.

*I'll tell you what – what about if you go and find your hidden room just like you want to. But before you do, I'll tell you what you find inside and if it's what I say it is, then you'll smoke the mixture and call on us and the right Legend will show you to where the amulet really is.*

No deal.

*Then you admit that it's not here?*

It could be here. Etienne was right that this Bridge was built at the right time. And Tamerlan had read about the rumors of a hidden room. If anyone could find that room, it would be Tamerlan and Etienne. Etienne had brought the book with them, and he'd given it to Tamerlan before he started to inspect the railing.

The book went into detail about the way the bridge had been constructed before moving on to Abelmeyer's mausoleum. Why detail the bridge if it wasn't connected to that somehow?

*I look at you and I laugh.*

Laugh all you want, Lila. I'm going to find the amulet.

*No, that's the clue about what you'll see inside.*

A clue? It sounded like a taunt. Tamerlan rolled his eyes and looked again at the bridge diagram. Why would they put that beam offset in one of the piers but not the others? That seemed strange. And the brickwork on that one – while the same in the diagram – looked slightly different on the actual bridge. He squinted at it. It was hard to see from up here. He needed to get further down the pier to be sure.

Down along the bridge, Etienne was trotting toward him. As the sun burnt the mist from the canals and the lower buildings, the people were pouring into the streets.

Dawning had always been one of Tamerlan's favorite holidays. He loved the feeling of setting your life in order, of cleaning out every part of it, of lighting your sins on fire to drift into the sky. They'd be doing that tonight, making little paper lights that drifted up into the air with their evil written on the balloons – setting it free, seeing it leave, cleaning out hearts and minds just as they cleaned buildings and streets. But this time during Dawning, that wouldn't be enough for him. His sin had flown up in the air, alright – in the shape of a dragon bigger than a city and more deadly than anything he could imagine.

And it seemed that Dawning was not the same this year in Xin, either. He didn't see the lines of Smudgers who usually filled the streets. He frowned as he looked around. Where were they during this holiday? He would have expected them to be there in huge lines of worshippers, weaving through the city. He caught sight of knots of timekeeper priests, their mandalas hanging from belts and cords around their necks. Their bells rang at their hems just as the bells rang every hour all through the city. But where were the Smudgers?

"We need ropes," Etienne said as he arrived back to where Tamerlan was. "There's nothing on the railings. The room must be somewhere below, and we'll only see it if we scale down from the top of the bridge."

"Where are the Smudgers?" Tamerlan asked.

Etienne ignored the question. "We can start with one pier and work our way down each of them to find where the secret room might be."

"It's here," Tamerlan said, tapping on the bridge diagram in the place where the architecture was just different enough to accommodate a small hidden room. The place he'd found by

141

looking at the book, rather than the bridge. But that was his way, wasn't it? He was a man of books, not of action. Or at least he had been before the Bridge of Legends opened.

*And now you are ours.* He shivered. He'd never get used to Lady Chaos' voice.

"I think you're right," Etienne said, his eyes glowing as he looked at the map. "There's room there. We need ropes."

"The Smudgers?" Tamerlan insisted. It didn't feel right that they were missing. There was something worrying about that.

"They left the city in droves, headed inland," Etienne said, his eyes still on the book.

"When?"

"When they saw the dragon in the sky." Etienne looked up and met Tamerlan's eyes. "I bet you never guessed that your destruction spread to other cities, too, did you?"

Tamerlan swallowed. "Why leave?"

"We don't know why. We just know that they did. Word is, they left all the cities that same night."

"I'll get ropes, if you have the coin for them," Tamerlan said in a defeated voice. He could burn all his sins in lanterns and never atone for them. He could rappel down high bridges and risk his life in foolish quests and none of it would ever be enough.

"I think that would be best," Etienne said, taking the book and handing him the coins he needed. "And maybe you should hurry before the rioting gets this far.

"Rioting?"

Etienne pointed toward the Trade District where the smallest pillar of smoke was beginning to rise.

"You don't know that's what's happening," Tamerlan protested. "It might be an accidental fire."

"Trust me," Etienne said. "It's rioting. And there will be more riots until the dragon is dealt with and the threat to the city is over." He looked Tamerlan in the eyes. "The threat you caused."

# 17: In Tune

*MARIELLE*

Marielle woke with a start.

"He left something for you," Allegra said with a wry look as she shoved Marielle off the foot of the bed. Condescension poured off of her like steam from a kettle, tinged a blush pink and stinking of day-old fish. "And you should stop falling asleep next to this man until you can decide how you feel about him."

"I feel pity," Marielle said thickly.

Allegra snorted, handing a note to Marielle. "Is that what people are calling it? In that case, you should bring a few refugees in from the cold. Dragon knows they need it."

Marielle blushed, looking at the note. It was folded carefully and had her name written on it in a swirling script. That wasn't what she expected Tamerlan's writing to look like.

"Anything to report?" Allegra asked casually.

"You saw Etienne more than I did," Marielle protested, opening the note. Surprisingly, it was from Etienne, not Tamerlan.

*Marielle,*

*I have need of your services today in keeping the Children of Queen Mer busy. Please give them my condolences. I will not be able to attend them today. And make a note of anything said or done. I will require a full report from you tonight.*

*Etienne*

Another person demanding that she report on someone else. By the time this was done she would be Chief Spy of Xin. She swallowed down a feeling of discomfort. She didn't want to spy on the Harbingers. She didn't want to spy on Etienne. Her options were narrowing like a closing window.

Allegra sniffed. "I need you out of the shop today. I have business to attend to."

"Do you mind if I spend that time in your inn?" Marielle asked. "The streets are too dangerous for Scenters right now."

"Spend it wherever you want, just not here," Allegra said.

Easy enough. With the Wind Rose aching over her heart, Marielle would have run to the Harbingers even without Allegra throwing her out, or Etienne assigning her to them. She needed to know about this magic that could amplify her gifts. She was thirsty for it.

By the time she reached the door to the suites of the Harbingers in the inn, she was already second-guessing herself.

What if they didn't want to see her? What if they had left? What if they decided she wasn't good enough to train – or worse, what if they took one look at her and knew she was a spy now?

She lifted her hand and knocked.

The door swung open so quickly that she nearly fell forward.

"You're late," Anglarok said, pulling her inside the room.

"Late? I- "

He shoved his big conch shell into her hands and guided her by the shoulder to one of the seats.

Across from where she sat, Liandari was sparing with two of the harpoon men, all of them soaked in sweat. Marielle felt a pang of sadness as she remembered sparring like that as part of her Jingen City Watch training. Sometimes even Carnelian would spar with her. And now she'd never spar with any of them again.

There was something different about this, too. The Harbingers didn't move the way Marielle was used to. They chose attacks she'd never seen before and those flowed into defenses she didn't know. Her eyes were glued to their movements. She could try that parry next time she had a sword in her hands. She could try that throw. The way Liandari had maneuvered under that harpoon was masterful. If she –

Anglarok cleared his throat. "Attention."

Marielle's eyes snapped to his face.

"We're not here to watch others work. We are here to work, too. Take the shell to your ear and tell me what you hear." He smelled of anticipation – spring grass colored swirls of cilantro twirled around him.

Marielle had heard of shells that made the sound of the ocean. She lifted this one to her ear as she voiced a question.

"Why do the harpooners never speak?"

There was a gasp from the two sparring with Liandari. Liandari flicked a finger and they froze in place.

"These are the nameless. They do not speak," she said.

"How did they lose their names?" Marielle asked.

The whole room was looking at her with shock. Eventually, Liandari swallowed and when she spoke, her mouth sounded dry.

"You don't have the nameless here?"

"No."

"Then how did you earn your name?"

Marielle felt her hands go clammy as she watched Liandari shift the grip on her weapon.

"It was given to me."

The room was so quiet, the horror on each face growing, that when the first sound in the shell rang in her ear, she heard it as clearly as if it were in the room with her.

147

The roar of a dragon filled her hearing, shooting straight into her brain and running like freezing water down her spine. She could feel her hands trembling as she held tightly to the shell, and then suddenly the room burst with rainbow colors – everything suddenly amplified in brightness as if the sound had caused them all to spring to fuller life. Liandari's suspicion roared through the room with bursts of bronze hope from the nameless harpooners. There was excitement flaring from Anglarok mixed with a smug satisfaction. And as electric blue sizzled through ribbons of bronze and apricot, Marielle thought she could make out distant voices.

"Hurry! Get out while he is resting. There's time to flee!"

"Dragon's spit, he'll see us!"

"Legends have mercy! Have mercy on me!"

She shook like a leaf in the wind, her heart reaching out to the voices ragged with terror. Who were those people? What were they fleeing from?

The looks of horror around her disappeared and the harpooners dropped to their knees, quivering while Liandari swallowed, visibly composing herself.

"I don't think we need to question her name, Ki'squall," Anglarok said quietly. "In all my years as Windsniffer, I've never seen such a powerful affinity."

Liandari took a deep breath, her face growing hard. "Why are you connected to this dragon, Marielle? Did you open the Bridge of Legends? Are you the one we seek?" She stepped

148

forward, aggression in her movements and rose-tinted obsession in her scent. "Answer me!"

"I – I didn't open anything," Marielle stammered. She'd made the wrong choice coming here. It would have been safer on the streets or defying Allegra.

"Then why does the dragon sing to you? Why do you channel echoes of his magic?" Liandari smelled of violence.

Marielle stood up from her chair, clutching the shell like it could shield her somehow. "Echoes?"

"It's what the shells are for," Anglarok said simply. "They magnify magic, echo it, take what is already there and make it greater. We searched all night for the dragon. And we searched all night for the one who opened the Bridge, but we found neither."

Liandari strode forward, quivering with emotion. Garnet and pitch poured off of her in waves and Marielle flinched back.

"You are connected to this dragon somehow," she said. "That level of resonance is no mistake."

"We've shaved days off of our time to find him," Anglarok protested. He smelled like he was trying to defend Marielle. Instinctively, she drew back as he spoke. "We can use the girl to track the dragon down. It will save us time, and we will be honored when we return to the ships of the Retribution."

Liandari paused, the scent of strawberries rippling from her suggested she was thinking hard. "I still want an answer."

"I was meant to be sacrificed to the dragon, but at the last moment, someone ripped me away from the ceremony," Marielle said.

"'To be sacrificed'" Liandari quoted her. "'Was ripped.' Are you only a pawn in the hands of others or do you make your own choices? I thought you said you were not nameless. The nameless do as they are told, go where they are sent, are silent in the presence of the named. The named take their own initiative. They find, they seek, they choose, they do. Are you named?"

"Yes," Marielle said, her cheeks hot.

"Prove it. Make a decision."

Marielle swallowed. Liandari was right about her. She'd been pushed in a corner by Allegra, pushed into another one by Etienne. She'd been saved and set on this course by Tamerlan, but where was the last time that she'd made her own choice about something other than the Wind Rose? If she really cared about writing wrongs and setting the course of the world back on track, should she really be hiding in these rooms or should she be headed out to fight a dragon?

"I'll need the clothing of a warrior, and a better weapon, supplies for a week of travel, a solid boat, and this shell," Marielle said as boldly as she could. Was she really doing this?

"And?" Anglarok prompted.

"And the help of someone who knows how to follow this resonance."

Liandari smiled. "Good. The Ki'Tempest will be pleased. We will locate this dragon before the end of Dawnspell and bring him the head of the creature on a pole."

Marielle looked around the room and swallowed. Seven of them to one dragon. What could go wrong?

Liandari snapped her finger and three of the nameless gathered their cloaks and belt pouches and left.

"We'll set out when the supplies are ready," Liandari said. "Work with her, Anglarok. See if she can find the one who opened the Bridge of Legends, also. Perhaps we will be shown double favor."

Marielle swallowed. What had she gotten herself into? She was no Legend swinging a sword and slaying dragons, but it seemed like she might need to be just to survive. She didn't think that Liandari took the word "no" very easily.

# 18: Rope and Riots

## TAMERLAN

Tamerlan scrambled along the canal toward the Temple District. He'd run out of coin to hire a gondola and the rope was heavy, but this was still the most direct route back to the bridge. Besides, the edges of the canals were still relatively safe – not like the streets. He clamped down on the anxiety that filled him at the thought of the streets. Etienne had not been wrong about riots.

By the time Tamerlan had made it to the Trade District to find rope, there was enough smoke in the streets to make anyone worry. On top of that, bands of men and women surged through the choking smoke, weapons in hand and grim looks on their faces. He'd watched a group of them grab a pair of Xin City Watch Officers. They were tying them in rope by the time he left, and he didn't want to know what they'd do after that. He itched to stop them, but how did you stop half of a city?

It had taken long minutes and more coin than he would have liked to convince the shop owner to sell him rope. Every shop in the District was barring the doors and windows when he went by. Those who could go indoors were inside. The streets felt eerily familiar. They felt like they had on Summernight in Jingen. He swallowed down the memory.

"Where's the Eye?" he'd heard the mob asking the Watch Officers. As if they had some hidden clue. "Tell us!"

What would he and Etienne do if they found it? If they kept it hidden, this would only get worse. If they revealed it, they'd be torn apart for it.

The citizenry weren't the only ones who had gone crazy. He'd narrowly dodged a pair of men in military garb only to see another man grabbed by them and hastily tied to a long chain of other men.

"Recruiting for the Xin City Army!" one of the men in uniform called as he tied his victim to the chain. "If volunteers cannot be found, recruits will be culled from the populace to fill our quota! Join the army here!"

He shuddered at the memory of that. Only Lila's sneaky suggestions had coached him out of the thick of things with his skin intact and still out of uniform.

"Tamerlan!"

He spun at the sound of his name, sagging with relief at the sight of Jhinn rowing along the canal.

"Jhinn!"

"Hop in the boat, boy. What are you doing with all that rope?"

Tamerlan leapt from the side into the little boat, rocking side to side as he regained the balance he'd lost as he landed.

"I … I couldn't find you before, Jhinn," he stammered. "I don't know how to thank you. You saved my life!"

"I might have just saved it again. This city is in bad shape," Jhinn said, pointing to where the Trade District was going up in plumes of smoke. "Setting fire to boats. Theft of property. Dumping waste into the canals. It's disgusting. We should move on. Find a different city."

Tamerlan laughed. If only he could. But he sobered up quickly. Just because he needed to atone for his sins didn't mean that Jhinn did.

"You should go, Jhinn. Pick anywhere but here. You should go somewhere safe. You don't owe me anything." He paused, feeling guilty. "I owe you everything, but I can't pay you back. Not yet, at least."

"None of us is promised anything in this life, Tamerlan. Nothing but adventure. And I've had a few. But now that you are real again, you should come with me. Leave this horrible place and find a better one."

Tamerlan scrubbed his hand through his hair. "I can't leave – not yet. I have to find an amulet and use it to stop the dragon. I owe the world that. All the destruction that dragon caused – it's all my fault."

Jhinn shrugged. "You didn't make the dragon. You didn't build a city on him."

Tamerlan sighed. "If only it was that simple."

"And the rope?"

"We're looking for the amulet in the *Dragon Collar Bridge*."

"I don't think there's any treasure hidden in that bridge," Jhinn said critically. They were in the lock now, working slowly upward toward where the bridge spanned the canal. It soared high above them, a marvel of modern engineering. Tamerlan swallowed. He couldn't see the variances in the bricks from here and he was starting to doubt that the amulet would be there.

*Because it's not.* Lila Cherrylock's voice rang loud in his mind. Behind her voice were echoes of Ram – always close to the surface.

*Dragon. Dragon. Dragon.*

"You should smoke that stuff. I have all your herbs hidden and I bet that those spirits could help you find the amulet," Jhinn said quietly.

He wasn't going to smoke it. Not ever again.

*We'll see.*

"They seem to think you're wasting your time with the bridge," Jhinn said with a shrug.

"You can hear them, too?" Tamerlan asked wide-eyed.

"Sure. Can't you?"

"I thought I was the only one!"

Jhinn shrugged again like it wasn't important. "They're dead people talking. So what? Dead people talk all the time. They call to me from the shore. Sometimes they offer coins even before they become real."

How strange would it be to live life thinking everything on dry land was not real? That it was owned by the Satan?

"Just smoke the stuff," Jhinn said. "Stop wasting your time."

"I can't do that," Tamerlan said with trembling hands, examining the bridge piers as he spoke. "Last time I chose to do that, I did terrible things."

"Because you did it in the world of the Satan. Do it in my boat. I'll row you out into the sea. What harm can you do out there?"

"I could hurt you," Tamerlan said reluctantly.

"Those spirits aren't going to hurt me," Jhinn huffed. "The red-haired one just winked at me."

Tamerlan put a hand over his eyes. How embarrassing.

But Jhinn's plan was solid. What could it hurt to try it out on a boat far from people? Maybe he would get added insight that way.

*Do it!*

Was that all four legends speaking at once? Tamerlan shivered at the thought.

"Okay, but we'll have to sneak out of the city into the river or out to sea," he said nervously.

Jhinn grinned as he rowed the gondola out of the lock and to the side of the canal where a small jetty allowed gondolas to offload passengers.

"Good. I want to fish. There isn't a scrap of food in this Mer-forsaken city! Do you know the message tree near where I dropped you and Marielle off?"

"I can find it."

"Go there tonight and I'll be waiting. And if you find any food, bring it. I'm hungry."

"Thanks, Jhinn," Tamerlan said, leaping from the gondola with his coils of rope. Whatever Lord Mythos had done had healed him completely. He hadn't felt this good in a long time.

The thought of trying the smoke again with Jhinn out on the ocean filled him with relief. He *did* want the knowledge and power that only the Legends could give him, but he didn't want to hurt anyone. This was the perfect solution. What could possibly go wrong?

# 19: Sins of the Father

*TAMERLAN*

The winding steps up to the top of the bridge gave Tamerlan a long time to think. With his health restored, sneaking away tonight wouldn't be too difficult. It would be the best course, really. A contained experiment. He'd have to make plans to keep Jhinn safe. Maybe if the boy held Tamerlan's sword – yeah, that might work.

There were few people on the steps – and no wonder. Tamerlan's feet were dragging before he reached the top. Fish sounded like a good idea right about now. Maybe Jhinn was right that they should spend a little time fishing.

The bells began to sound the next hour, clanging and tinkling, pounding and pealing. They were so familiar. He'd been hearing them his whole life on every Dawnfast since he could walk.

He used to like Dawnfast – not the actual fasting of course, and not the part where he was constantly nagged for daydreaming when he was supposed to be cleaning, but he loved the purification of it. He loved the sense of being washed from the inside out and made new to face another year. He loved imagining Grandfather Timeless marching forward with the world balanced in his panniers. What must that look like?

He was almost at the top of the stairs – his eyes drifting over the city below, rolling out from this high point of the city, district on district, his mind floating on visions of Grandfather Timeless – when his gaze caught on Etienne. The young man – dressed head to toe in black like a brooding raven – motioned to Tamerlan to join him and as he waved to him, the other men talking to Etienne turned to look a Tamerlan.

That wasn't –?

No.

It couldn't be,

Tamerlan froze midstride as a familiar pair of blue eyes caught his. A cruelly familiar face – handsome and chiseled – but cloaking a malevolence most people never saw – smiled slightly at the sight of him. It wasn't a smile of welcome on the face of that tall, broad-shouldered man. It wasn't a smile of fatherly affection. It was the smile of a chess player happy to see one of his pawns returned to the board.

Tamerlan shook himself and forced his steps forward. It was too late to run. Too late to hide. He'd have to face this like a man. He lifted his chin with determination, clenching his jaw until he was close enough to speak.

"Decebal," he said. There would be no "father" from his lips. His father lost that privilege when he sold Tamerlan to the Alchemists.

"You nearly killed me, son," his voice was cool. An icy sheath over a sharp sword. "I didn't think you were half that skilled or I would have sold you to the army for a much better price."

"You lived," Tamerlan said, shocked by how hard his voice sounded. "How?"

"I took your sister through the secret passages below the Seven Suns Palace. They lead out under the walls of the city – a short path to the land beyond Jingen. Most of the Landholds with any sense went that way. Next time you plan to destroy a city and everything in it, you should plug up the ratholes if you don't want the rats to escape."

"That was never my intention," Tamerlan said, angry at himself for the heat he felt forming in his cheeks. He wasn't a child anymore. He owed this man nothing. Why did he feel like he needed to explain that this wasn't his fault?

Etienne cleared his throat and Tamerlan almost felt grateful when the other man raised a narrow eyebrow, though he had some explaining to do. That was not the account he had given of how Tamerlan's father escaped the city.

"You know Decebal Zi'fen, and of course you must know Renli Di'Sham of Yan, soon to be his son in law and Renli's brother Han Di'Sham," Etienne's voice was calm. "We owe Yan a great debt for their generosity in taking in the refugees of Jingen."

160

"We aren't here for introductions," Decebal growled. "We're here to make sure that you understand our terms. You will renounce your role as the Lord Mythos of Jingen, fold Jingen and her Landholds into the governance of Yan as we ask."

"And if I do not?" Etienne asked calmly.

"You are a Myth-Keeper without a Myth. A lord without a city. A man without a home. You are nothing but an empty name."

"Then why does it matter to you that I renounce it?" Etienne asked, leaning against the bridge railing and looking out across the city to the horizon where Jingen still smoked in the distance. By moving there, he had turned his back on the men speaking to him.

Tamerlan shifted awkwardly. Their words were daggers and if Etienne wasn't careful, he'd be getting a real dagger in the back. If they were asking this, then they had plans for the title of 'Lord Mythos.' Tamerlan glanced quickly at his father. Was it possible that Decebal wanted the title for himself? Could he be thinking of restoring Jingen with Yan's help now that the chaos surrounding the city had ripped power from every other hand? It sounded like something he would plan.

"Why keep a name that only mocks you every day with what you lost?" Decebal asked.

"Is my sister well?" Tamerlan interrupted.

Decebel looked shocked at the interruption, but it was Renli who answered. "She's safe and well, though shaken by her brush with death."

161

The look he gave Tamerlan made it clear whose fault he thought that was. And he was right, of course. Amaryllis' terror, this political maneuvering, the smoke in the distance, the riots springing up across Xin – none of these things would have happened if Tamerlan hadn't smoked and become Ram the Hunter.

So, why did it feel so urgent that he try it again?

*Yes!* A voice echoed in his head. *Try again!*

But Tamerlan's father had already moved on. He leaned in close to Etienne so that Tamerlan could barely catch his words as he hissed.

"Your power is gone. Your authority has ebbed away like a receding tide. Even Lady Saga did not listen to your request not to make this year's Dawnspell Hunt about the amulet."

Lord Mythos met him look for look. "And how is that working out for the City of Xin?"

Decebal spat, his next words loud enough for all of them to hear. "And now here you are, a weak fool, still clutching to the trappings of a life you lost. By next week, no one will remember your name."

Decebel left them – lackeys at his heels – with a flurry of shaken capes and rattled swords.

"Like birds, strutting for attention," Etienne said with a single raised eyebrow before nodding to Tamerlan. "Not going to change sides now, are you?"

"To serve the Satan?" Tamerlan asked, watching his father leave. "I think not."

"He's no Satan. Just a petty man with petty wishes. He wants power, but power is not a thing you can hold. It's a lion on a chain. You have to make sure it is always feeding on something else, or else it turns around and feeds on you."

Tamerlan shivered, dropping the heavy rope to the ground. "Where do you want to tie to?"

It turned out Lord Mythos was fussy about knots – a good thing considering that he'd decided Tamerlan would be the one to go down the rope.

"You need someone up here to make sure no one dislodges the rope while you climb. Someone with authority," he said by way of explanation.

Tamerlan didn't bother rolling his eyes. Why expect anything else? Etienne was just as addicted to power as anyone else. As long as there was someone to command, he'd be commanding them.

Tamerlan took a deep breath, adjusting the safety rope that Etienne had helped him tie around his thighs and waist. It tied to the bigger rope already hanging down the wall. All he had to do was lean back, walk down the wall, and pull the knot of that safety rope down with him as he went, and he would be fine.

Yeah. All he had to do. No big deal.

The canal below swam in his vision as he took a deep breath, his belly lurching at another glance below him. This bridge was way too high for this kind of thing, and Tamerlan was way too queasy in high places. He was already sweating as the nerves took hold of him. But what choice did he have? It was his idea to look in the pier and if the Legends were wrong and the amulet really was there, then it was his duty to find it, collect it, and use it to bring down the dragon he'd let loose on the city. He took a deep breath and slipped over the rail.

"Don't look down," Etienne suggested casually. He was holding Tamerlan's sword in his hands as if he expected to be attacked at any moment.

Why did advice always sound like someone drunk was giving it? How could Tamerlan afford not to look down? He couldn't exactly do this safely with his eyes closed.

Gritting his teeth, he leaned back, back, back until he was perpendicular to the pier of the bridge, his rope creaking as his weight grew heavier against it. The ropes were secure on the rail. He knew that. He'd seen Etienne tie them, but now that his life depended on them, it felt like there weren't enough, like the rope wasn't strong enough, the knots not firm enough, the day not sunny enough.

Enough complaints! With a strangled sound he'd never intended, he took his first step backward – or down – or whatever. So far, still alive.

Another step.

He tried to focus on the traffic on the bridge. It was picking up now that mid-morning was upon them. Primarily foot traffic rather than carts or barrows like you would see in the working areas of the city. Were those clusters of people with drawn, hungry faces their fellow seekers of the amulet?

"Ho!" he heard one of them call to Etienne. "What are you doing with that rope?"

A cluster of well-dressed young people joined the first man, but now the breeze was picking up, catching their words and whipping them away as Tamerlan descended lower and lower. He was watching for that anomaly in the stonework – though what he'd do after that, he didn't know. There hadn't been any hints on how to open a secret room – if there was one.

His steps were growing shakier. Maybe he wasn't as recovered as he thought he was. He didn't want to look down to see if he was getting close to the patch of stonework. That would be a mistake. Any glance below would probably make his head spin right about now. Instead, he focused on one step at a time.

Etienne looked small, the crowd around him growing, when Tamerlan finally saw the stonework right below where his feet were planted.

Okay. Now what?

He took another step back, his foot on the strangely cut stone. It pressed in, and he stumbled slightly, the safety rope tightening as his feet slipped into the divot. The stones around the sunken one sunk with it until he was knee deep in the pier.

Wha-

There was probably enough room to crawl into that hole – if he dared.

*You'll have to. It's the only way in.*

Wow. A little warning would have been great, Lila.

With gritted teeth, he sunk into a crouch until he was waist deep in the stonework, twisting so that he could hang his legs into the pier, balancing on his belly instead of his back.

*There is a ladder. But you'll have to untie yourself.*

No way. The rope was the only thing keeping him alive.

*Don't be such a kitten. Just do it.*

With a sigh, he carefully loosened his safety rope until he could untie it and slip further into the hole.

Dragon's spit in a cup! He eased his legs lower, seeking a rung with his feet. Lila had better be right about this!

His toe caught something, and he sank his weight onto it, grimacing while he did, his heart pounding in his chest. It was too dark to see if she had been right.

Carefully, he ducked his head, curling into the hole the rest of the way, his second foot looking for the next rung and finding it. He was slick with sweat now, forced to wipe his hands on his clothing so they wouldn't slip.

Next time, Lord Mythos could do the climbing.

His eyes were adjusting to the dark. There were small openings in the stonework that lit the ladder he stood on, but his perch

166

was so precarious that he couldn't twist to look below him. He'd have to climb the rest of the way down. With a barely-suppressed moan, he climbed slowly down the ladder – it wasn't a real ladder, just stones sticking out enough to make rungs. No side rails to hold with his hands. No security to keep him from slipping. Every step was a gamble.

By the time he reached the bottom, he was trembling. All his muscles felt like jelly.

The wooden floor felt – bouncy. Not a good sign. Water must seep in through the cracks in the stone that were his only light source, damaging the wood.

He turned carefully, trying not to move too quickly. He didn't want the floor to fall out from under him.

Stone beams went from the walls to the center of the room in a sunburst pattern. Tamerlan hurriedly moved to the nearest one, stepping up onto it. That was better. Less chance of falling through a rotting floor.

With his heart in his chest, he balanced along it to the center of the room where a small platform stood with an iron chest at the center. This was it.

No matter what the Legends said, it felt like the amulet *could* be here. After all, what else would be in a hidden chest in a hidden room half-way down a massive bridge?

His pulse raced as he reached the platform, reaching to open the heavy iron lid of the chest. It fought him – the hinges rusted and seized. With a great heave, he wrenched it upward, looking into its velvet-lined depths.

There was something there! Something that glinted red!

He reached inside and pulled it out.

A mask, lacquered to look like a white face with red curls of hair around it and a winking eye, stared back.

*Told you so,* Lila said. *Deathless Pirate says he's the one who last touched the Eye. If he can be believed. I don't ever trust pirates.*

Defeat tasted bitter on his tongue.

# 20: In a Flurry of Dust and Wind

Marielle wrapped her scarf around her nose a fifth time, surprised that Anglarok didn't do the same as they strode through the city toward the river. If he had the same skill as she did, shouldn't he be equally sensitive? The stink of Xin was becoming overpowering to Marielle. To anyone else, it probably felt fresh and clean. The streets were being mopped now that the sweeping was done and the even the tile roofs were doused with buckets of water by anyone not on the hunt for the amulet.

Tonight, all of Xin – and everyone else throughout the Dragonblood Plains – would celebrate the second night of Dawnfast. They would write their sins on paper balloons, light the candles at the base of the balloons and watch them float off into the sky to burn away and leave them clean. Already, she saw people in houses constructing their own balloons while street vendors laid them out with their other wares to be purchased for that night. Each one was white – a symbol of purity – though they would be gold when they were lit – a symbol of the burning justice of the heavens eating up the sins of the people.

Marielle had bought one of the balloons, using a small coin she'd had in her boot. She probably should have saved it for food along the journey, but her need for forgiveness was more pressing than her need for food.

Judging by the stink of guilt and rage – twin scents twisting through Xin in a garnet and cranberry fog – the rest of the population needed forgiveness, too.

Marielle choked as a fresh surge of fog hit her. A group of hard-eyed soldiers marched past with a long line of men and women chained together. The rage radiating off the captives and the guilt of the soldiers lit aflame her own rage and guilt. They ratcheted up higher with every whiff of it that she smelled.

"Xin will not stand by while the dragon is loose!" one of the soldiers called to her, but he didn't stop. The glance he exchanged with the other soldiers told Marielle that he knew he didn't have enough allies in a fight against her and the Harbingers.

That deep guilt worried Marielle. It was as deep as her own and she had the blood of thousands on her hands. She had the pain that went along with that, searing deep under her skin so that she felt like she was burning all the time. What had they done to match her guilt?

The intensity of the emotions around her spiraled upward, as out of control as a forest blaze, so that one person's rage fed their guilt and spread to the next person sparking rage in him even as his own guilt pushed him to spark it in someone else. There was no end in sight, no fresh rains or dousing water to quell what was happening in Xin. Marielle's only hope was that tonight when their sins went sailing upward, they would burn up with the lanterns and burn their rage and guilt up to nothing until forgiveness rained down on them like the ashes of the sky lanterns.

Her eyes teared up as she thought about it, following Anglarok with glassy vision. He escorted the Ki'squall, guiding Marielle with nods and looks to keep her in the right place in the formation. Around them, the nameless fanned out, weapons on display, grim faces and silence better deterrents than even the harpoons they held.

"You have no place here, outlander!" a man from the crowd called, stepping in front of them. He stank of drinking and desperation – a pulsing orange mixing with a dove-grey fog of dulled senses.

"Move on," Liandari said with a tight voice. Her close-cropped hair shone in the noon sun and the expression on her dark face was deadly. "You don't need trouble."

"Maybe I want trouble," the young man said. He twirled a barrel stave in his hand like a weapon. "Maybe I want that Scenter of yours for my hunt."

Marielle pulled her new sword from her belt, but before it finished rasping from the sheath, Liandari had already leapt forward, her dark double-breasted coat swirling where it flared around her legs, her hands so fast that Marielle didn't see her sword move until after the man's head was already rolling along the street, his body slumping in slow motion to hit the cobblestones with a heavy thud. Anglarok kicked the head, flipping it into the nearby bucket of cleaning water where it bobbed in a grisly warning to anyone else who might want to pick a fight with them.

Marielle's breath caught in her throat as Liandari flicked the blood from her blade.

"Anyone else?" she asked quietly.

The crowd backed up. No one else wanted to tangle with Liandari.

"I like this city," Liandari said casually to Anglarok. "I get such little sword practice in the Isles. Live duels are always more effective than planned ones with practice blades, don't you think?"

"Mmm," Anglarok said, his gaze sweeping across the street before them as he hunted for threats. In all the violence and rage, Marielle didn't know how he'd sniff anything specific out at all. She was having trouble scenting anything else, her nose overpowered by the scent of smoke, pitch, and cranberries.

She carefully sheathed the sword they'd acquired for her and looked down at the clothing – leather and wool, fashioned for someone of much more noble blood than the daughter of a red-door woman in the Trade District of Jingen.

Maybe she should have emphasized that the clothing should be practical. She'd thought that went without saying, but the elaborate woven-metal decorating her leather breastplate and carefully wrought clasp at the center of her chest was anything but practical. Sure, it would protect from attack, but she looked like a Legend with all the decoration – polished metal scrollwork and leaf decorations swirled in ways that emphasized her femininity while also looking foreboding enough that she was surprised anyone had tried to kidnap her. The greaves and gauntlets – also leather – had swirling feathers worked in metal decorating the fronts of her calves and forearms.

She felt over-dressed, like she drew the eye too much, but Liandari had smiled when she presented them to Marielle and right now, Marielle didn't dare offend her benefactors.

She wished she'd had a chance to say goodbye to Tamerlan and Jhinn. She owed them that much. But this was her best chance at making things right – and at squirming out of the tight corner that Lord Mythos and Allegra had shoved her into. It would be hard to report on people if they were both in a different city than her.

In the distance, the canals were packed with gondolas, barges, and family boats. They worked their way through the busy streets toward the nearest canal and Marielle worried more with every step. If it was this crowded in the canals here, how bad would it be as they moved upriver toward Yan? Would there be refugees scattered across the countryside? Was her mother out there, perhaps, walking to safety one step at a time? Her breath caught in her throat as she thought of that.

"When we get to the barge that will take us upriver, we will talk more about what you can hear in the shell," Anglarok murmured. "We must find where the voices are coming from, track them if we can to the place where the dragon has settled. It's essential that we find him."

"Of course," Marielle agreed. She wanted to find the creature, too.

Someone jostled against her and she stumbled to the side, surprised to see a knot of young women carrying weapons and wearing eyepatches.

"What are you looking at?" one of them asked her. "We're the Band of Abelmeyer and we're the ones who are going to find the Eye!"

"Dragon-speed to you," Marielle said politely, glad that her scarf hid her incredulous look. The whole city had gone mad.

They were coming up on the Xin City Smoke House, a tall tower billowing with spicy smoke. In Xin they did their meat smoking in the Spice District instead of the Trade District. It made sense. After all, the spices they needed were here, but she wasn't the only one smelling delicious smoked meat during a time when the whole city was fasting, and she probably wasn't the only one getting more and more irritable because of it. She could smell it even over the rage and guilt of the city and that was saying something! Her mouth was watering, and her eyes began to tear up, too. How long had it been since she had a decent meal? She'd had food on the boat with Jhinn, but she wouldn't call that a meal.

Her mind drifted back to eating fried meat pies with Carnelian before Summernight. Was that her last hot meal? She felt a little faint as she remembered it, her memory of Carnelian – the betrayer – so strong that it brought back the smell of the dragon with it. Funny how memories evoked smells.

She could smell the cedar musk of a nearby dragon so strongly, it was as if the dragon was there. She shook her head. She needed to keep her mind focused on what she was doing, not drifting to the past.

A scream erupted from the crowd and Marielle froze, looking around her. Anglarok and Liandari were crouched, weapons already drawn. The harpoons of the nameless were out and ready as they spread out in a ring around their leaders.

But there was nothing else. No more screams. No clash of weapons.

Marielle began to relax as the crowd around them returned to motion. Just a false alarm made worse by her imagination. Fool! She should be keeping her mind on her task, not on useless memories.

A second scream ripped through the air and then the people on either side of her began to flee toward the alleys and doors of the buildings on either side of the street as a dark shadow blocked out the light.

Marielle looked up just in time to see the belly of a dragon overhead.

He was close – far too close – and on his wings and back and neck ruined buildings and roads were still crusted like a layer of barnacles he hadn't been able to scrape off.

He let off a cry like a gull – but deeper, more guttural. It shook the earth under Marielle's feet. No. Wait. It shook the dragon deep down under the road under Marielle's feet. Or at least, it seemed to her that was what was happening.

Her heart was in her throat. The seconds dragged out like years. She braced herself, her sword held high – as if that could do anything to a creature so large. How had she ever thought they could kill such a monstrous creature?

Each flap of its wings was so powerful that people tumbled down the street as if caught in a hurricane. Stalls selling wares, carts, oxen, and small buildings upended and somersaulted down the streets.

Marielle thought she might be screaming, but the sounds around her were so deafening that she couldn't hear herself. Screams and shouts, the sound of wood shattering and stone crumbling created a cacophony so loud that words were lost in the torrent.

Terror filled the air – vinegar scented, burning the nose, tinting everything with raw red.

The dragon's massive head dipped down, and he seized the towering Smoke House in his mouth, tearing it from its foundations like an uprooted plant. Stone and earth rained down from the tower.

Marielle scrambled backward, colliding with one of the harpooners. Her vision was blocked by whirling bodies, fleeing in terror. She saw a stone the size of a cart fall from the sky, crushing two of their harpooners at once. Saw Anglarok lean over them, shaking his head. A scream caught in her throat.

Liandari sprinted forward but a cart, hurtling down the street, smacked her in the back, sending her spinning through the air to land on the ground in a crumpled heap just inches from Marielle.

Marielle jammed her sword in the sheath. It was useless to her right now. She leaned down over Liandari. Was she still alive?

She heard a scream from behind her and she turned in her crouch just long enough to see a piece of masonry fly past. It was the size of a small house. It flew past inches from her head. A warbling ripple of insensible terror pulsed through her.

If she'd still been standing ...

She shook her head to clear the thought. Not time for that.

She pulled Liandari up, dragging her by her upper body through the rubble of the street. Her veil slipped down, and the scent of acrid fear and musky dragon, tinged with cedar, smacked her in the face.

She made it a full pace before a piece of masonry as large as she was smashed down onto the street where Liandari had been only moments before. Marielle's mouth fell open, her body freezing as she tried to grasp what had just happened. Anglarok was there in a moment, lifting Liandari's legs and pointing with his head to an alley already filled with people.

"There, bring her there," he shouted, his words barely audible above the noise of the street.

Marielle struggled against the wind, fighting to keep her footing as they worked their way to the mouth of the alley, pushing their way into the crowd there.

She thought she saw looks of protest on the faces there – this alley was already too full – but it was too loud to hear their words, too bright a red to see any other scents.

They huddled together in terror until, at last, the winds stopped, and sound returned to their District.

"I don't think we'll be leaving the city just yet," Anglarok said grimly when he could be finally heard. Marielle nodded in agreement.

In the street, the rest of the harpooners lay dead, struck by that block of masonry that had narrowly missed Marielle.

And as they stepped out from the alley, plumes of smoke filled the sky in every direction.

The dragon had returned.

Xin was no longer safe.

# 21: Black Plumes

### TAMERLAN

By the time he was up the rope again, Tamerlan's arms were on fire, his fingers tingling like he was losing circulation. He'd never climbed up a rope like that before. Certainly not without having eaten for days before. His head swam and his throat was dry when his hand finally reached up and grasped the top of the railing.

A pair of finer-boned hands grabbed his, heaving him over the railing where he fell in a slump. Oh, Legends, he was exhausted.

*Yes! Call on us! Let us take you!*

When he was weaker, they were louder.

*We come when your strength fails, when your mind needs to be faster, your endurance stronger. Why do you deny us?*

He could barely keep their voices apart in his mind as he fought his exhaustion.

179

"Drink this," Etienne said, shoving a flask in his hand. "Stand back!"

Etienne's legs were inches from him, almost as if he were standing over Tamerlan.

Tamerlan gulped down the water from the flask, his head clearing a little as the cold refreshment of water spread through him.

They were surrounded by a crowd of people, people with weapons and intent expressions. They looked like they were waiting for something, all their eyes trained on Tamerlan as if he were the salvation of their souls, the deepest joy of their hearts. He shivered.

"Well?" Etienne asked tightly.

Tamerlan reached into his shirt and pulled out the mask. It laughed at him even now.

"What is this?" Etienne hissed.

"Show us! Is it the amulet?" A voice called from the crowd.

"Come on!"

"You promised to show us!"

Etienne was looking at him with a grim look on his face, shaking his head. He whirled around, raising the mask up in the air as Tamerlan struggled to his feet.

"Behold!" he cried. "The treasure!"

"It's just a mask!"

"That's no amulet!"

"What is it?" a girl in a pretty red cloak asked quietly.

"A joke," Tamerlan said and the crowd stilled, listening.

"It's not very funny," the girl said.

"It is if you're Lila Cherrylocks," Tamerlan said wryly.

Etienne shot a warning glance back at him. But it wasn't like Tamerlan was giving anything away. Lila hadn't been lying about the mask, and that meant she wasn't lying about who really had the amulet last. She'd said it was Deathless Pirate. That, he would keep to himself.

He heard her name ripple through the crowd.

"Lila Cherrylocks."

*Yes! They call to me! They speak my name! Keep telling them of my wonders, alchemist!*

At least he'd made someone happy.

*I might know...*

"She stole it many years ago," Tamerlan said. "And now her mask mocks us in our hunt."

"Lila," the crowd muttered, but there were sparks in their eyes. By tonight, every place Lila had ever visited in the city would be ripped apart as they looked for the amulet.

*My glory increases! My renown is great!*

181

He shouldn't tell anyone else about her. She liked it way too much.

*Haven't you heard?* She said, slyly. *Our power increases with the renown of the masses. I should have been smart like Grandfather Timeless and founded my own religion. Then I'd really be powerful.*

Tamerlan didn't even get to think about what she might mean. At that moment, a gasp rippled through the crowd. Etienne spun, his face filling with horror as he looked past Tamerlan.

Tamerlan spun just in time to see a guard tower along the southern wall go up in flame as the dragon sped toward their city.

"Jingen," he gasped and Etienne echoed him.

Etienne rocked forward, his hands gripping the railing as he leaned forward. Whatever he was trying to do had no effect, but even with the dragon still far away, the wind of his wings made Tamerlan's cloak flap in the wind behind him.

"We need to get off this bridge," he said, loudly enough for everyone to hear. "His wings alone might destroy it!"

There were screams from the crowd and Tamerlan heard the sounds of hurrying, but though he tugged at Etienne the other man wouldn't move.

"Come on! We'll die here!"

"This isn't working," Etienne said, fists clenched and brow furrowed.

"Tell me about it!"

182

Tamerlan looked back at the approaching dragon and then at Etienne. Whatever magic he was trying to work wasn't doing anything at all. And the man was going to die if he didn't move. The wind of the dragon's approach was already making it hard to hear his words.

Gritting his teeth, Tamerlan grabbed his belt knife, slashed the safety rope around his waist, sheathed the knife and then turned to Etienne. He'd have to act. The other man was too obsessed with whatever he was trying to do.

Grabbing the smaller man in a bearhug, Tamerlan pushed forward, knocking Etienne off his feet and then hurtling to the nearest end of the Bridge.

Screams filled the air around them.

Tamerlan glanced over his shoulder in time to see the dragon's head plunge down into the city and snatch up a tall building up in his jaws, cracking and crunching it, as masonry fell from his jaws. Houses and streets still clung to his back, bits of their structures raining off of the creature like dust from a shaken mat.

Tamerlan gritted his teeth, his heart pounding in his head as he turned his back on the dragon completely and plunged forward toward the end of the bridge. The structure was shaking under his feet, swaying with the wind of the dragon's every flap.

He followed the screaming crowd toward the heart of the University District, his feet pounding on the wavering ground, his arms trembling as he bore the other man to safety.

When his feet finally found street cobbles and left the bridge. he stumbled to a halt, releasing Etienne.

Behind him, a cracking sound met his ears and then the sound of rock on rock. He spun to see the center of the Bridge cave in.

There wasn't time to investigate or wait for the next thing to happen.

"Come on!" he yelled, plunging toward where the buildings were the thickest, where maybe, possibly, they could escape the devastation of the winds.

Tamerlan dove into the first narrow alley he found, turning to help Etienne in behind him. He stayed anchored in that spot, bucking the high winds and reaching out pulling in one person after another to this tiny shelter until suddenly, there was a powerful force of air pushing down on them and then nothing.

Nothing but silence and sobs and ringing ears.

They stumbled out of the alley together.

It was hard to see very far into the city here among the clustered buildings, but one thing was easy to see – plumes of smoke filled the air in angry black swirls.

The dragon Jingen was back.

Their time to stop him was running out.

# 22: SPIRAL TO DESTINY

*TAMERLAN*

It was long hours before they reached Spellspinner's Cures again. Long hours of helping to douse fires, gather the injured, and clear the streets. The hunt was on hold. Every face that Tamerlan and Etienne passed was full of wariness. Was the dragon going to return? Had this only been the beginning? The same question rang in Tamerlan's head as he looked up to the sky every few minutes.

But the dragon had not returned, and the city had slumped into quiet waiting as dusk descended.

They opened the doors of Spellspinner's Cures to a burst of voices and bustling people. Women in white aprons trotted briskly across the shop floor carrying bowls and pestles, jars and bales.

Allegra glanced up from her counter with a harried look in her eyes. "No room for you here today. Go next door. Marielle will sort you out."

"Can we help?" Tamerlan said, sagging against the doorpost.

She snorted. "You're in no state for that. You should be in bed. But your bed is full. Every bed is full, and the storeroom besides, and I have orders for poultices and feverfew and healing teas from every District. Two untrained fools would only get in the way." She wiped her brow wearily before her eyes narrowed again. "Out!"

Etienne pulled Tamerlan away and to a small door in the side wall.

"It adjoins with the inn," he said tiredly, leading Tamerlan through a long corridor and up a flight of stairs to a door that looked like every other door in the hall. Even in the inn, a quiet hush had fallen.

Etienne knocked while Tamerlan watched the hall warily. He'd seen sorrows today that he wished he could forget. People trampled in terrified crowds. The ruins of people's livelihoods. A child's shoe left in the middle of one street had him the most worried. What had happened to the child? Was he safe – or was he one more victim of this madness?

And over it all was a tone of guilt and urgency. Guilt, because he was the one who freed Jingen and started all this. Urgency, because he must be the one to end it.

He'd meet Jhinn tonight. Together, they'd try to call the Legends and find the amulet. He swallowed down the thought that it might be worse to call them than not – after all, they were the ones who had landed him here. But what other option did he have? The dragon was the size of a city. Nothing short of magic would stop it now.

He just needed to get away from Etienne's watchful eyes. He'd have to wait until the other man was sleeping.

The door swung open and Marielle's eyes grew wide at the sight of them. Her dark hair was rumpled, little strands of it loose around her face, and smears of dust were on her forehead and around her eyes. The bottom half of her face was clean – protected by the scarf that hung loosely around her neck. Her breeches and white shirt were torn and dirty.

Tamerlan paused, captivated by the sparkles in her purple eyes. No matter how frazzled or ruined she looked on the outside, those eyes were always bright and intelligent. He'd know them anywhere. He wasn't sorry that he'd saved them. He was sorry for everything else, but not for that.

"The Harbingers?" Etienne asked, pushing past him into the room.

"Liandari is resting in her room," Marielle said, pointing to one of the closed doors as she shut the main door behind them. "And Anglarok is tending to her. Her head was injured in the attack. Allegra says she will recover, but she hasn't woken up yet. The nameless ... the others ... died in the dragon attack."

Etienne nodded briskly, patting her on the shoulder. "Tamerlan and I will take their rooms for tonight. We have work to be about tomorrow."

He was all business, striding off to the door Marielle had pointed to. Marielle's eyes trailed after him as if she were hoping for more, but there wouldn't be more. Tamerlan and Etienne had failed to find the amulet.

"This is yours," Marielle said, after a long moment, reaching into her boot and pulling out a folded piece of paper.

Tamerlan took it, but he didn't want to look at it. He didn't want to take his eyes off her tragic beauty for even a moment. He'd seen too much ugliness today. Why couldn't he just enjoy something beautiful for a moment?

Even rumpled and disheveled there was just something about Marielle that enchanted him. Maybe it was the curve of that top lip of hers that seemed to be begging for a kiss. Maybe it was the way that she always seemed to be standing on her tiptoes, leaning forward, like a hunting hound sniffing the air for the quarry. Maybe it was the looks she gave him – sharper than a knife. She was edges and curves, alertness and softness, focus and forbiddenness all folded into one.

Even now, as he looked at her, he saw her as someone else, a great queen rising up out of the sea. A Legend walking – a winged helmet on her head, and angel wings on her back, and a bright sword in her hand. The foam of the sea would pour off her head and drip down her long hair and her eyes would sparkle as the sun rose behind her. She would say something strong about justice and truth and raise her sword and all men would gather under her golden banner.

"Tamerlan?" she asked, an edge to her voice.

"Mmm?" And he would stand at her side, her protector and guard, happy to lay down his life in her service.

"What are you staring at?"

He blinked, the vision melting away.

"Nothing. Sorry." He could already feel his cheeks heating. Now was not the time for daydreams. He looked down at the paper she had handed him. It was the recipe from the ancient book – the one that had started it all. He was a little breathless when he spoke. "Where did you find this?"

"In your rooms in Jingen. When I was investigating you. I thought that perhaps you would like it back."

He swallowed, looking up to give her a gentle smile. "It was kind of you to keep it for me. Will you hold on to it a bit longer?"

"Why?" she asked, moving to the wide balcony on the other end of the room.

Tamerlan followed her, looking out across the city as the last glimmer of gold slipped down over the horizon. Choking smoke hung over the city, but in the distance, the first fire lantern went up, a tiny firefly spark in the distance. The first sin burned up. The first hope of redemption sent up to the heavens.

After a moment, Marielle slipped back into the rooms, but Tamerlan was riveted to the balcony, his eyes searching hungrily for the next lantern and the next and the next. If only life was so simple. If only everything could really be forgiven just because you wrote it down and burned it up.

Marielle slipped in beside him, her footfalls soft. She carried paper balloons and candles.

"Do you want to celebrate Dawnspell with me?" she asked, a look of wariness in her face.

"Yes," he said. Perhaps, she would slay him with her gleaming sword one day. Perhaps her justice would be his redemption – her hand the executioner's. He'd embrace that if it ever came. But for now, he would write on paper and send it to the sky with the last shreds of hope he possessed.

He didn't know what she wrote on her paper lantern. He didn't sneak a peek at it as she lit the candle and sent it up. Whatever guilt Marielle carried could not be very heavy. She'd done nothing in her life but live for good. She'd even been willing to give her own life for Jingen. She was innocent.

He put his charcoal to the paper and in big letters, covering the balloon, he wrote one word. One word that summarized his guilt and shame. One word for which he would never be forgiven. No matter how many prayers he sent up, no matter how many tears he shed. And with a sigh, he lit his candle and watched the orange glow outline the word he'd written as the fire lantern sailed into the sky to join the thousands of others just like it.

JINGEN.

His shame.

His sin.

"I swore an oath to justice with Queen Mer's People," Marielle said as if confessing some great hope. "They gave me a tattoo."

Tamerlan felt a ghost of a smile playing around his lips. He remembered seeing that tattoo peeking through her collar when she slept – so sweet, so caring – at the foot of his bed.

"I'm going to find King Abelmeyer's Eye," he said in return. And it felt like a vow more than a confession. Because anything he said to Marielle in that moment would have felt like a solemn vow. She was the avatar of goodness.

"I think they know what justice is," she said. "They came here for it. It's why their ships are waiting. They're waiting for news of where to strike. Where to bring their retribution. And I want to be on the side of justice."

He nodded in the orange glow of the tiny lanterns floating above them. More sailed into the sky as the people of Xin pled with the heavens for absolution.

"I just want to stop that dragon. I just want to make the world safe again," he said, feeling like he was still standing on sacred ground, so close to his shining muse.

"Do you think a person can find redemption in this life?" Marielle asked him.

It was so much like the question he'd asked her yesterday. And as she looked up at him with desperate eyes, he wondered why she was asking *him* that. She'd already told him that she didn't think he could be forgiven. Was it possible that she thought she needed to be?

"You have no need of redemption, Marielle. Nothing that happened on Summernight was your fault. That was all mine. All of the guilt rests with me," he said gently, smiling down at her worried expression. Boldly, he reached forward and brushed the loose hairs from her face. She flinched back. But he didn't let his smile waver. "And if you did, I am certain you would be given it."

Her smile was sad – almost reluctant.

"I'll hold onto your paper," she said, reaching for it. Was that all she could give? Perhaps. Perhaps she couldn't ever forgive him, but she could do this one thing – a small favor. A small gesture.

"Thank you," he said, as he held it out to her because he was grateful that she hadn't mentioned all the things she couldn't give.

His heart lurched a little as she strode away, closing her door behind her. She deserved redemption – wherever she got it. She didn't even need it. Only the foul needed their sins atoned for. Only the bloodstained. Only people like Tamerlan.

With a sigh, he went into one of the empty rooms, quickly cleaned up and reordered his things. He'd wait a few minutes before he snuck out. A quick rest and then he'd go out hunting his own redemption.

# 23: Hunting Redemption

*Tamerlan*

Tamerlan's arms shook as he opened the package Jhinn handed him. They'd slipped through the locks and out to the river and into the Bay of Tears without a glance backward.

"Are you sure you want to do this?" he asked again.

"Just do it, boy, and stop whining about how dangerous it is," Jhinn demanded. "I have your sword, don't I?"

He did have Tamerlan's sword. He was holding it in both hands as he waited for Tamerlan to smoke the herbs and transform into a Legend.

*Come on! Do it!* That was Byron Bronzebow. And behind him was the never-ending chant that sounded behind Tamerlan's every thought, *Dragon. Dragon. Dragon.*

If obsession had an avatar, it would be Ram the Hunter.

If only he could choose which Legend came through and took him over. It would be easier to do this if he knew.

*There are ways to push the balance more to one of us or the other,* Lila said in his mind.

Now she told him! How did he do that?

*Ha! I'm not letting that slip yet. Not until I'm sure that it's me you'd be choosing.*

Well, that was no help. Tamerlan swung the door open on the lantern at the front of the gondola and carefully lit the end of the little paper tube holding his herbs.

"I can't believe you kept so many safe," he said to Jhinn right before he sucked in his first puff of smoke.

"Are you kidding me? If you died, I could have sold them for a fortune," Jhinn said.

Tamerlan shivered. Imagine selling them! Imagine setting these loose on the street where anyone could use them however they wanted! The thought made his toes curl and his stomach lurch. He pulled in another puff.

"Maybe hold onto that roll-up this time, yeah?" Jhinn said. "I bet you could keep the spirit around longer if you puffed on it again half-way through."

It wasn't a bad idea. Although the Legends tended to have a mind of their own about what they were going to do.

Dark waves lapped against the gondola and the bright moon picked out the silver edges of the waves as Tamerlan waited for the smoke to have its effect. The breezes were warm, but the smoke still lacing their edges set his teeth on edge.

*Hunting treasure, are we?* A wheedling voice asked.

He should be used to this by now, but as the Legend took over his body, Tamerlan shook inside. Legends send he didn't murder Jhinn! Legends send he didn't destroy anything!

*I don't slaughter my sailors. Then I'd have to do the rowing.*

He'd actually gotten Deathless Pirate! He'd wanted him, and here he was!

*Sometimes that can help. Sometimes it doesn't matter. But no one calls on the sea without me listening.*

Did that mean he'd always get Deathless Pirate if he smoked on the sea?

*Don't think you can control us, boy. We aren't birds perching on your shoulders. Now, what are we doing out here and what treasure do we seek?*

Was Lila right? Could Deathless Pirate really know where King Abelmeyer's Eye had been hidden?

*Abelmeyer's Eye, is it?* Cackling filled his mind. *It's always some trinket that men want. Some object that glitters in the sun. Trust me when I tell you, they don't last. That is, unless you hide them. I can take you to where the Eye is. Oh yes, I can. I stole it just like Lila says. And I hid it in my cave of treasures. And now that you mention it, I might like to see if the other things hidden there are still ... secure.*

Really? For once he wasn't going to have to ride in the mind of a Legend who wanted something drastically different from him! For once, he could actually work with the one who came.

*I don't take orders from anyone. I do the ordering. But yes, today we are of an accord. Our interests align. Let's go find this treasure.*

"Boy," Tamerlan heard his own voice saying, but it was Deathless pirate controlling it. "We appear to be in the Bay of Tears. Is it so?"

"Sure," Jhinn said, lowering the sword.

"And do you know of a small flat island about a half of a league from the shore just out from Dragon Spit Point?"

"Bare Island?" Jhinn asked. "Sure."

"Let's row there now, then, aye boy? And we'll see what we will see."

Jhinn shrugged.

"You do the rowing," Tamerlan said, "and I'll do the steering."

Jhinn paused, clearly reluctant to leave his beloved boat in Tamerlan's inexperienced hands, but after a moment he shrugged again and moved to the oars.

It was maybe an hour of hard rowing – all from Jhinn – before they reached the small island. He'd better puff more on the roll-up or Deathless Pirate could disappear before they got further than the island.

*Is that the way of things? Then keep these coming.*

They puffed on the last bit of roll-up before tossing the ash into the sea.

"You've been followed," Deathless Pirate said in Tamerlan's voice. "First rule of pirating – don't let them see where you're going."

Tamerlan tried to see what Deathless Pirate was talking about, but the world beyond the light of the lantern hanging from the ferro of the gondola was dim, and even in the light of the full moon, the shadows were long and inky.

*But don't worry about your mistake, boy. I will be here long enough to teach you better. Now that you've taught me your little smoking trick, I think I'll stick around for a long time. They call us Legends. They look to us with fear and longing, worship our power, flinch from the consequences. We do not flinch. We do not waver. We do not wonder what it would be like to have this kind of power. We learned long ago how to get what we want. And what I want is life. And I want to live it through you. And think about it, boy – can't I do more with your life than you can? I've heard your foolish cries for redemption. No one needs redemption. What you need is to embrace yourself, your goals, your desires. Together, you and I are going to do that.*

And just like that, their goals were no longer aligned.

*Oh, we'll get the Eye. I'll give you that much.*

If only he'd laid out other ways to signal Jhinn. Jhinn wouldn't suspect anything was wrong unless they threatened his life and Deathless Pirate seemed to like him.

*All good Captains need seamen to follow them.*

He should have thought this through better.

Their boat hit the shore, skimming up on the flat white sand of the island. Clumps of loose grass grew throughout it, white driftwood piled in tangled heaps to one side and, bird dung was everywhere. But there was nothing else here. No trees. No pool of water. No structures. Not even rocks. Just a flat skiff of sand that was probably invisible during high tide.

*Yep.*

"I didn't bring a shovel," Jhinn said casually.

"No need," Tamerlan heard himself say. "I buried layers of coconut fiber mesh under the sand. It covers this entire island. It holds the water and you can't dig through it. Shovels are as useless as wishes on *Bare Island*."

"Did you think you could sneak away?" an authoritative voice asked as a second boat skimmed up the sand.

Jhinn's jaw tightened, but Tamerlan didn't even feel Deathless Pirate flinch.

"More treasure hunters," he said coyly with Tamerlan's voice.

Lord Mythos frowned. He was dressed in fresh black, a wide satchel slung over his shoulder and a hired boatman at the stern. He must have followed Tamerlan the whole way. Had he used magic to disguise himself? He claimed not to have it anymore, but he had used it to heal Tamerlan.

"You can join me – for a price," Tamerlan heard his voice say. Lord Mythos' frown deepened. He glanced at Jhinn and then back again.

"I thought your price was redemption?"

"Redemption doesn't fill a treasure cave, now does it?"

"I'm just here for the Eye," Etienne said. He leapt from the boat, tossing the boatman a leather purse. "I'll return with these others. Thank you for your work."

He shoved against the prow of the boat, launching it back to the sea as Deathless Pirate leapt out of his own boat.

"Let's see how good you are at claiming it, hmmm?" Deathless Pirate challenged.

Don't kill him. Please don't kill him! Tamerlan thought desperately.

It was strange not to have the other Legends in his mind, but now that he was possessed by Deathless Pirate, their voices had disappeared. Even Ram's constant refrain was gone. If he wasn't so worried about what Deathless Pirate was up to, he would have found it a relief.

"We'll make a game out of it," Deathless Pirate said. "Whoever finds the Eye first, keeps it."

The Lord Mythos was silent, regarding him warily as Tamerlan laughed in a pitch just a little too high and then took off, striding across the island.

Anyone watching Tamerlan right now would think he was insane. Jhinn and Etienne probably did. He shouldn't have risked this. He could have found the Eye on his own.

*Oh no, you wouldn't! A pirate's lair has traps. And the first trap on this lair is the tide. Lucky for us, it's low tide right now, or we'd have to wait for the tide to change and on an island this boring I might resort to torturing one of these fine companions just to pass the hours.*

Tamerlan gritted his teeth inside. This was the kind of thing he was worried about. He'd have to let Deathless Pirate take control of the hunt or risk seeing Jhinn hurt just to entertain a ghost.

# 24: MAP OF DEEDS

*MARIELLE*

Sleep did not come for Marielle. She didn't even try. She sat on the edge of her bed, staring at the recipe on the page Tamerlan had asked her to hold and thinking about what he'd said.

He liked her too much. She wasn't sure why he'd decided that she was valuable. Why had he saved her back in Jingen? Why did he tell her now that she didn't need forgiveness? Why did he have to be so beautiful and such a devil all rolled into one? A silken-tongued tempter and a blood-slicked murderer. A sincere, hopeful boy and a man who'd seen too much.

Tamerlan was complicated and Marielle didn't need complicated right now. She needed solid things.

She shivered as the word 'solid' brought back the memory of solid blocks of stone whirling through the air and sweeping people off their feet, crushing them, battering them, destroying them. Her life since the beginning of Summernight had been nothing but chaos and destruction, death and tragedy. Perhaps, when Jingen rose into the air, the world had actually ended?

Perhaps she was just living in the dried-out husk of what had once been the world.

A knock on her door sent her leaping to her feet.

"Come," she said, a little breathlessly, stuffing the paper back into her boot.

Anglarok opened the door. He was bent with weariness and his clothing was dirty and torn.

Marielle spoke first. "Would you like me to take a turn watching over Liandari?"

"It is not honorable to trust the care of the Ki'Squall to anyone not of our people," he said.

Marielle nodded, not knowing what to say.

"You saved her life." Maybe it was hard for him to concentrate on just one thing. After all, he'd just lost four companions and his leader's life was still in jeopardy. "That makes you honored among us."

Anglarok dropped to his knees. Marielle gasped, reaching forward to steady him, but he waved her away.

"Honored one, please receive from me this gift in payment of the debt of honor we owe you."

He held out a shell – a conch, like his turquoise one, but this one glowed a canary yellow with a sparkling silver rim. Again, she couldn't determine its scent and yet she could see colors with it. It was small enough to fit in her palm. A quarter of the size of his other conch, but still magnificent.

"I can't," she protested. "Really."

He drew a knife from his belt, lightning fast, his face hard. "Then, take what you are owed."

"The knife?" she asked, confused. It looked almost as valuable as the shell. Carvings of ships in high seas covered the aged ivory handle and the blade was sharp.

"My life. As her Windsniffer, it is my duty to pay her life debt. You may take my life in return for the one you saved, or you may take an object of equal value."

He was joking, right? But he didn't seem to be joking. He seemed to be deadly serious.

Gently, hoping that he wouldn't suddenly lunge with that knife at either her or himself, Marielle reached for the shell.

"You think this shell is of the same value as your life?"

He nodded. "It is smaller and untested, unbonded, but it has the same potential as the conch I carry. The magic it contains is worth more than a single Windsniffer life."

Marielle swallowed. Was it more troubling that he held his own life in such poor esteem or that he was offering her a magical object for no other reason than that she'd saved a life? She would have done that for anyone.

"When someone saves a life," Anglarok said, as if explaining to a child, "the value of that life belongs to the one who saved it. If it is not purchased back, then the work and life of that person will belong to the savior. The Ki'Squall must not be in your debt. That is why it is my duty for the sake of her honor and my own to buy her life back from you with my own, or with an object of equal value. It's a matter of the Real Law."

And there it was again, this Real Law that she never seemed to be able to nail down.

"I would be honored to accept the conch shell," Marielle said as formally as she knew how. No one was going to die just because she had saved Liandari, and no one was going to be a perpetual slave, so accepting this gift seemed like the best option. Even if Jhinn had warned her not to accept anything. Even if she was more than a bit nervous that it had a color in her monochrome vision without any scent attached to it. "Thank you."

The gift left her shaken. She'd just been thinking about Tamerlan and the undeserved regard he'd showed her. And now the most honorable people she knew were telling her that she owed him the debt of her life. What gift could she give him of equal value to her life?

"And there is the matter of recording your honor," Anglarok said, standing finally. "Come, we'll do it together as we watch over Liandari."

"Recording?" Marielle repeated, trying hard not to stare at the conch. It was so beautiful that she was having trouble looking away from it. She kept it in her palm as Anglarok led her to Liandari's room and sat with her in the chairs beside the bed where Liandari lay, insensate.

"Your Wind Rose was the start, but we record the maps of our lives, a representation of everywhere we have been with honor.

You conducted yourself with honor in this city today, so today we will add this city to your map."

"You mean you're adding to my tattoo?" Marielle asked, feeling the sting of the one she already had as she spoke. She hadn't been prepared for additions. It gave new significance to the tattoos all over Anglarok's skin.

"Yes. It is a matter of honor."

And what could she say about that?

# 25: OPEN EYES

*TAMERLAN*

Deathless Pirate had taken complete control of Tamerlan's body and Tamerlan could feel his exuberance in the way he ran across the sand island.

*I haven't been this young in a long time.*

He'd yanked the gondola lantern off the ferro before he went – much to Jhinn's irritation – and was scrambling over the sand island, the lantern bobbing with every long stride. He was looking side to side, though what he could be looking for was beyond Tamerlan. The island had no clear shape, no structure, no trees or rocks or anything to make any part of it stand out.

*Many have sought my treasure, but I did not make it easy to find.*

He reached the other side of the island quickly, Etienne following in his footsteps.

"Where are we going ... Tamerlan?" Etienne asked, pausing before using Tamerlan's name, almost as if he suspected that was not who he was really speaking to.

"Under the side of the island. Only good for low tide," Deathless Pirate said through his mouth. His voice was breathless with excitement. "Why don't you come? We'll show you a sight you've never seen, hey?"

"And the lantern?"

"Good construction. Made to keep water out. Should burn long enough to get us there."

Etienne shivered, but Tamerlan was already stripping. Great. The Legends never seemed to care much about his modesty. They dressed – or undressed – him like a doll they played with.

He was down to his smallclothes before he knew it, tossing his clothing at Jhinn with a laugh.

"Hold onto these for me, sailor!"

Jhinn mock-saluted with a saucy expression but the look in his eye was sharp. Did he see the spirit? Did he know Tamerlan was possessed? Probably.

"Ready?" Deathless Pirate asked, but he didn't wait for Etienne to finish undressing. He waded out into the water.

One step. There was cursing behind Tamerlan as Etienne struggled out of his clothing.

Two steps.

"Hurry or you'll lose him!" Jhinn urged him.

The sand shelf dropped suddenly and Tamerlan plunged into the water, sucking in a deep breath the moment before his mouth and nose were submerged.

The pirate had better know what he was doing! He'd better be a good swimmer. Tamerlan could swim, but he wouldn't say he was expert at it.

*I'm an expert at most things – all things, if we're talking about the water. One month on my ship and I'd make a man out of you, too. Your hands are lily soft.*

He was kidding, right? Tamerlan's hands were calloused and worn from his work as an apprentice.

*Not like they'd be if you were hauling on rope all day!*

But now Tamerlan was too distracted to argue with the Legend. They were sinking deep into the water, only the light of the lantern showing the way. The rock of the island was porous with great big bubbles on the surface of the rock. Strange.

Tentacled creatures fled from the light and the edges of fins or tales would flicker briefly along the edges of the lantern glow. Tamerlan mentally shivered at the thought of being down here without the lantern. What would it feel like to have those tentacles brush his leg? Or wrap around his neck?

Deathless Pirate seemed unconcerned. He located a small hole in the rock almost immediately. It was small – no wider than Tamerlan's body. He'd better not try to wiggle into – no! No! No!

Terror gripped him as Deathless Pirate plunged the lantern ahead of them into the tunnel and then shoved Tamerlan's shoulders into the narrow space. He was too wide! His shoulders too thick! He'd never fit!

*Stop whining. Or I'll send you for twenty lashes to sober you up! You'll fit. You have no belly. It's just the shoulders to maneuver.*

Which wasn't making him feel any better. Sharp rock dug into his shoulders and chest, scraping and ripping painfully at his skin.

Something grabbed his foot and fear shot through him like an arrow.

*It's just that skinny one – the one in black who followed us. He can't see the light of the lantern with all your bulk in front of him.*

Etienne. Okay. At least he was human. Mostly.

And now his lungs were burning, and his heart was racing. There was no way he could get to the surface in time to fill them!

*You need to develop more tolerance for holding your breath.*

No way he could back up through the cavern in time, either. He was almost wedged as it was, and Etienne was behind him. This had been a terrible idea! He would die possessed, not even in control of his own decisions that led him to this place!

*Forty lashes unless you spare me!*

The tunnel bent upward suddenly, widening and as soon as his shoulders shoved into the wider tunnel, he shot upward, his hand with the lantern leading the way. It was flickering, but still burning.

His hand broke the surface, the lantern flaring brighter, and then his head broke through and his burning lungs gasped in stale air.

It had been so close. He'd almost died!

*You would have died if you were piloting this ship, but lucky for you, I was at the helm.*

Etienne burst up through the water, sucking in his own deep breath. The look he gave Tamerlan made it feel like he'd been weighed and graded in the Trade District.

"What is this place?" he asked.

"My lair," Deathless Pirate said grandly, spreading an arm. "But take a care. There are traps."

They scrambled to the edge of the pool where a rock lip – smooth but rippled like it was made from water rather than stone– spread out around it. The smoothness went up far above them, but rough steps were carved into the rock leading above.

"When the tide is high this is all much more difficult," Deathless Pirate said, running a hand over Tamerlan's face to wipe the water away.

"I imagine that's the charm of the place," Etienne said dryly.

"Indeed!"

Deathless Pirate was already sprinting up the stairs avoiding every third one. Hopefully, Etienne was noticing that. It seemed to Tamerlan that the pirate was snickering inside far too much for that not to be a trap.

They raced up the steps and Tamerlan heard Etienne bite back a curse. It must not have been too bad, though, because his footsteps were still right behind them.

The stairs topped out just above the high-water mark, and then they were in the cave.

"You can hide out here if you really have to," Deathless Pirate said aloud almost as if he was musing to himself. "There are holes in the rock that I drilled in there when I made the place. They let air in and out at low tide and you can close off the doors at high tide. No food or fresh water, obviously, and you can't fit the whole crew, but in a pinch, it will do."

Tamerlan wasn't listening to him. He was gasping mentally at the treasures laid out on shelves and spilling out of chests all around the room. Deathless Pirate's eyes skimmed over them as if taking inventory. Diadems and coronets crusted in jewels, long sabers with gem-encrusted handles, and ivory carvings lay on shelves or stood in racks. Jade statues made to look like dragons, lions, octopuses, and a thousand other creatures were decked in pearl necklaces, or emerald pendants. Vases with scenes of battle inlaid in their walls stood neatly in rows.

It was everything a treasure room should be.

"Touch nothing," Deathless Pirate said, breathless as he surveyed his wealth. "The wrong weight on any shelf will open a sluice and fill the cavern with water."

It must have been difficult to get so many heavy, priceless things in the cavern.

*I put them in here before I sealed the island up with the coconut fiber. We dug down to place them here. Some of those chests wouldn't ever go through that cavern. Even you won't fit if you put much more muscle on these shoulders.*

"And the Eye?" Etienne asked from behind them. There was tension in his voice as if it were all he could do to stay frozen in place in front of so much wonder.

But as he said the words, Tamerlan's eye caught a single ruby the size of a human eyeball. A flaw in it made it look like a narrow pupil resided inside it – shaped like a cat's pupil. Or a dragon's. He gasped at the same moment that Deathless Pirate laughed. The Eye hung from a fistful of chains wrapped around each other to make a cord thicker than both Tamerlan's thumbs put together.

"That has a special protection. I knew that someone would want it. Which means you might be out of luck, little man," Deathless Pirate said, grinning widely at Etienne.

"And why is that?" Etienne asked carefully.

"I rigged the protections on that one with magic – cost me enough, that's for sure! – and they can only be dispelled with magic."

"What kind of magic?" Etienne asked. Tension sang in his voice.

Deathless Pirate eased past the items on the shelves to a small fissure in the rock to one side. In all the wealth before them, Tamerlan hadn't noticed the fissure before. It glowed softly – a blue glow that flickered like light beaming through water. Deathless Pirate moved carefully around the shelves to make sure he didn't bump any as he leaned toward the fissure.

"Blood magic. Only a drop of blood from the Dragonblooded will release the amulet from where it sits. But you don't look like you have the blood."

"I don't," Etienne admitted.

Deathless Pirate leaned forward until his face was right in front of the fissure.

"What's that?" Etienne asked, carefully inching forward until his face was pressed up against the fissure, too.

Someone had set glass into this part of the rock and through the glass, you could see through the dark currents of the ocean to where someone had sunk a tall man-sized iron cage. It sat on a slight angle from where it struck the ocean floor. So close to the island, the floor was shallow, close enough for them to clearly see the cage, clearly see the blue light glowing from what was within – close enough to see the man with eyes wide open and a look of horror on his face. His clothing wafted gently in the current. His long black hair swirled in the motion of the sea. But his hands were frozen where they clutched the bars. His mouth frozen in a rictus of pain and his eyes frozen wide.

His flesh had not deteriorated or been eaten by fish. If he wasn't so still, Tamerlan could have sworn he was alive.

Tamerlan's mind shivered in horror. Someone had sunk this man and he hadn't died.

"You can't kill avatars," Deathless Pirate said in his voice. "You can only trap them. And when they are finally free, they roam the earth again."

Tamerlan tried not to think. After all, Deathless Pirate could read his thoughts. But it was no use. His own voice whispered the words he was trying so hard to avoid.

"The time has come for me to stride once more on the tide of man."

Tamerlan gritted his mental teeth. He never could have predicted this possibility. Letting one of the Legends out into the world of men would be so much worse than just letting them out to play from time to time through the Bridge of Legends!

He felt a sting of pain and then Deathless pirate was whirling as Etienne scrambled back, the tip of his knife dripping with blood – Tamerlan's blood. Dragonblooded blood.

He gasped as Etienne flicked it onto Abelmeyer's Eye, snatched up the Eye, and tore out of the treasure room and down the stairs.

With a roar, Deathless Pirate chased after him, lantern in hand.

*You didn't tell me you were of the blood!*

He hadn't asked.

By the time they'd reached the stairs, Etienne was diving into the pool. And by the time they reached the pool, the lantern flickering, he was out of sight. Tamerlan sucked in a huge breath and then dove down. He tried not to feel panicky at the thought of making this swim a second time. After all, hadn't he done it once before?

He was surprised that Deathless Pirate was chasing the Eye with such fervor. After all, he'd seemed taken with the idea of freeing his avatar.

*Fool! Don't you realize that the Eye has the power to bind and free? Why do you think I wanted it in the first place? It wasn't like I was interested in helping you toward* your *petty goals! I was always here for what is in that cage. You should have told me you were Dragonblooded!*

They pushed through the rock, Tamerlan wincing at the pain as the sharp edges bit and dug into his skin, the brackish water stinging his open wounds.

But as they reached the end of the tunnel, he began to feel his limbs growing clumsier. His lantern clattered against the rock as he took control of that hand again.

*Watch it —*

Deathless Pirate's voice faded from his mind and then he was left with one arm sticking through the entrance to the tunnel, the other shoulder wedged so hard he didn't know how to free it. He fought at the wedged shoulder, dropping the lantern, and in the descending dark his lungs lit on fire before everything went inky black.

215

DAWNSPELL

THIRD DAY
OF
DAWNSPELL

# 26: HAIL THE CONQUERORS

### *TAMERLAN*

Tamerlan's eyes opened to darkness. He sat up, sucking in a huge, fearful breath before he realized he could see the silver moon outlining everything around them. He wasn't underwater. He wasn't dead.

"I see you've returned," Etienne said. He was dressed again in the black clothing he favored and pulling on one set of oars while Jhinn pulled on the other set. Around his neck hung the Eye.

"We got it," Tamerlan said sagging in relief.

"Yes, we're quite the conquering heroes," Etienne said dryly. "And the magic is finally dissipating. Whatever trick you pulled back there did not make you a very likable person."

Tamerlan glanced at Jhinn who shook his head.

"No," Etienne said, "Your friend didn't give you away. But I have eyes and ears, and – shockingly – a brain to operate them and enough experience with magic to read the residues. I recall

218

a text I read back in my school days in the Queen Mer Library – a library which unfortunately is no longer with us."

Jhinn shoved Tamerlan's clothes toward him with a toe and Tamerlan smiled gratefully, pulling them on as Etienne continued. It was cool in the sea breeze and he was shivering as he dressed. The sword was even back in its scabbard waiting for him. He wished he'd grabbed one of the other treasures to give to Jhinn while he was in the cavern. Adventure might be what Jhinn sought, but it didn't pay for bread.

"It was an ancient text," Etienne continued. "A text about the Legends. You know the ones – like Deathless Pirate whose treasure trove we just plundered? And this text seemed to suggest that there was a special magic that could access them – the Bridge of Legends. How this could be done was unclear, only that it would take someone who had skill with herbs. You were an alchemist's apprentice before the fall of Jingen, weren't you, Tamerlan? I seem to recall that being a feature of Marielle's investigation. I remember visiting the room of the Butcher of the Temple District and seeing herbs there."

Tamerlan swallowed, focusing all his attention on dressing. He didn't want Etienne to notice how rattled his words made him.

"And when you spoke to your father earlier it was clear that the two of you are well educated. I remember that Landhold Zi'fen contains an excellent library. Have you also read of this Bridge of Legends, Tamerlan?"

"I don't recall reading a book about anything by that name," Tamerlan said lightly. It was the truth, though not the whole truth. The recipe for the Bridge of Legends had been a single page, not a book. Was Marielle keeping it safe?

Tamerlan finished buckling the sword belt on his waist and looked out to sea. Or rather, toward Xin. They were just outside the locks for the city, cruising through the quiet of the pre-dawn harbor.

"How long was I out?" he asked.

It was Jhinn who answered. "Etienne saved you from drowning. He says he pulled you from a cavern."

Tamerlan looked at Etienne's smug expression. He forced a smile in return. "Thank you."

"When you threw up all your water, I left you to sleep a bit," Jhinn said. "You're going to need sleep if the two of you go to trap that dragon."

"Thank you," Tamerlan said again, this time more sincerely. He owed Jhinn debt upon debt.

Etienne was tucking the Eye into his coat now that they were close to the locks.

"We'll keep this between ourselves," he said briskly.

"All of it?" Tamerlan asked. But why would Etienne tell anyone his secrets?

Etienne lifted a single eyebrow. "Perhaps."

Dawn had broken by the time Jhinn pulled up to the side of the canal and Etienne hopped out.

"We need to talk in private," Tamerlan said in a low voice before he left the gondola. Etienne was waiting, but what he wanted to say to Jhinn couldn't be said here and if he left Etienne alone he was afraid that the other man would slip away with the Eye and Tamerlan would lose his chance to stop the dragon and make right all his wrongs. "Meet here again in an hour?"

Jhinn nodded and Tamerlan trotted after Etienne. He never looked back once, striding purposefully through the waking streets to Spellspinner's Cures. He opened the door and Tamerlan barely managed to duck in behind him before it shut.

"Where were you?" Allegra, still fully clothed, practically ran from behind the counter toward them. Her face was flushed, and dark rings were under her eyes. "We were all set. The timing was perfect. And you were nowhere to be found!"

Her gaze was fixed on Etienne who glanced purposefully at Tamerlan. "We can talk about this later."

"We will talk now." Her words sounded like a threat.

Etienne dodged her grasping hand, slipping through the door to the inn, but Tamerlan was not so lucky.

"You owe me, too," Allegra said. Last night she'd practically driven him away when he tried to help and now she was demanding repayment?

"Yes," Tamerlan agreed and her eyebrows rose.

"You admit it."

"Thank you for healing me."

He wanted to slip after Etienne. He was worried about what the other man was going to do with the amulet, but he *did* owe the healer. She'd saved his life.

"How thankful are you?" she asked, stepping in a little closer than Tamerlan would have liked.

"Umm … very thankful?"

"Thankful enough to do a favor for me?" She asked, reaching out to touch his shoulder as if she owned him. He stepped back into the counter, swallowing against a pressure in his throat.

"I guess it depends on what that favor is," he said, his voice wavering more than he would have liked. She reminded him of the crocodiles that sometimes swam along the brackish edges of the Alabastru River. The look in her eyes was cool and calculating as she looked him over.

His face grew hot. There was a creaking sound behind her, but he didn't look away. He was afraid of what she might do if he was distracted.

"Do you have any experience laying siege to a palace?" she asked sweetly.

"Not exactly. Although I did cause a stir the only time that I set foot in one." Why did everything she said sound like it meant things he didn't understand?

There was a rustling sound in the storeroom. No wonder. In a city on a fast, the mice probably looked to spices for some kind of a food source.

"Any experience charming your enemies?" Had she winked that time?

"None at all," he said clearing his throat.

"Etienne keeps squirming away, but I think you could be useful," Allegra said. Why did those words make his hands feel clammy?

"I'm sure I can't be nearly as useful as he is," Tamerlan said, his voice shaky.

She looked at him for a long time, his heart beating faster from fear with every second. She reminded him of Master Juggernaut. Not a bad man, but when he wanted something, he got it, no matter how many competitors stood in the way and no matter who tried to stop him. And he usually got it on the terms he wanted. Tamerlan had a bad feeling that he was being weighed and evaluated for sale right now. He didn't know how long he waited like that, but he didn't look up when the door squeaked again. It must not have closed properly the first time.

"I'll let you know when I have need of you," she said eventually, wetting her lips in a way that made him want to run in the opposite direction. "You should get some sleep. The inn will have breakfast wafers in late morning to break your fast."

Tamerlan's mouth watered at the suggestion of food. He was so hungry he could eat just about anything. The tiny honey wafers the city would eat today to break their fast wouldn't be nearly enough, but he'd take them and be grateful. Of course, right now, he'd just be happy to get out of Spellspinner's Cures with his skin still attached.

"Sleep well," Allegra said with a smirk.

He nodded quickly and hurried away from her, through the squeaking door. He was faster than those mice as he scurried up the stairs to the door of the suite and slipped inside. Marielle's door was ajar, and Etienne's was closed. Tamerlan crept to his door and knocked softly, hoping not to disturb anyone else. A familiar smell wafted from under the closed door, but Etienne only opened it a crack, just wide enough to see a sliver of his face.

"Wasn't saving your life enough, Alchemist? Now you want to disturb my sleep as well?" he asked.

"I want to talk about the amulet," Tamerlan whispered. "We need to use it right away."

Etienne looked around dramatically before asking dryly. "Is the dragon attacking the city?"

"No," Tamerlan said, irritation setting his teeth on edge.

"Then maybe it can wait an hour for me to take a quick nap. Go away and let me sleep."

"Do you promise that we can make a plan to destroy this dragon after you sleep?"

His tone was severe. "When next we speak, we'll talk all about it. I promise."

He closed his door and the sound of the deadbolt was clear in the silence of the inn. Either Tamerlan could wait, or he could break down the door. He sighed, rubbing the back of his neck.

Why was Marielle's door open? Had she left? He snuck across the suite and peeked inside. She lay sleeping, her hand stretched out as if it had held something, though there was nothing there. He closed her door carefully and snuck to his own room, stripping off his wet clothing and taking the time to hang them up before falling into the bed. He fell asleep the moment his eyes shut.

# 27: Empty Hands and Empty Promises

*MARIELLE*

Marielle woke with a start. A bang reverberated through her room as someone opened her door so quickly that it bounced off the wall. A half-naked Tamerlan stood in the doorway, breeches tugged on but the laces not tied, no boots or shirt or anything else on.

She sat up, leaping to her feet. She'd fallen asleep fully clothed, her collarbone still stinging from her fresh tattoo of Xin and the paper he'd given her – the illuminated page from an ancient text – clutched in her hand. It was gone now.

Her gaze raked across the bed. Had Anglarok come in here and snatched it? She'd been debating with herself last night when she fell asleep. She hadn't decided whether she should tell him that a clue to the Bridge of Legends had been right there in her hands. After all, Tamerlan had entrusted it to her.

"He's gone," Tamerlan said spitting a violent curse. His light-colored hair was darkened by water and the ripples of his muscles – while dry – were pebbled with gooseflesh in the cool of the morning.

Marielle rubbed her eyes, swallowing awkwardly. She'd seen her share of people dressing and undressing in the Watch Officers barracks, but they rarely burst into her room an hour after dawn. Light poured in through the window behind her and a tiny tinkling began the hourly bells as they sounded around the city.

Could he mean Anglarok? Had she lost her chance to make this decision at all?

She waited as the bells finished ringing, brushing off her own shirt and breeches and running a hand through her tangled hair. At least he didn't know that the page was gone, too.

"Who is gone?" she asked with careful composure as the last peal of the bells died off.

"The Lord Mythos. Last night we found Abelmeyer's Eye." His eyes were bloodshot from lack of sleep and he smelled of desperation – and worse, of the siren-sweet scent of magic that he'd worn when first she met him.

"You've been around magic," she said sternly. "What have you done?"

He was so beautiful – and so terrible – like a devil sent to the world to tempt and seduce her and then dance on her tattered soul. She pushed back the golden scent of attraction, refusing to give into it. He wouldn't be her undoing no matter how often he showed up half-naked and beautiful in her bedroom.

"I'm telling you what we did!" Tension filled his voice. "Me, and Jhinn, and Etienne stole the Eye from Deathless Pirate's treasure trove. Etienne claimed he needed to sleep for an hour, and locked his door, but now he's gone."

There was another scent now that he said that – a faint smell.

"Aniseed?" she said aloud as she tried to figure it out. "And something else. Something familiar … wait! There was aniseed on the page you gave me."

Tamerlan's gaze flitted around the room and then locked onto hers.

"Did you fall asleep reading it?"

Marielle looked at her bed and swallowed. She'd slept on top of the blankets. They were hardly even rumpled. But there was no page there. Someone had certainly taken it. If not Anglarok, then Etienne.

"Yes," she said. She scrambled onto the bed looking over the side. No page. It was gone.

"Come on," Tamerlan said, purpose filling his scent and swirling around Marielle, too, like a ribbon drawing her after him.

He was across to Etienne's door in a heartbeat, shoving against it. It was locked.

"Stand back!" He stepped back a few paces.

"You don't need to – " Marielle began but Tamerlan ran at the door, shoulder first. He crashed into it and with a loud splintering crack, the door burst open.

The next door in the suite opened immediately and Anglarok stuck his head out, piercing her with a look.

"Are we under attack?" he asked sharply.

"No," she said, her mouth dry at his violent look.

"Then keep silent and do not disturb us. I've only just soothed the Ki'squall to sleep." He retreated back into the room and shut the door quickly and silently.

Marielle breathed a sigh of relief and followed Tamerlan into Etienne's room. She could have told him that the room was empty. She hadn't smelled Etienne behind the door. What she did smell, was the exact same scent of haunting spices that she'd smelled in Tamerlan's room back in Jingen. She spun, looking at him as he stood alert in the doorway, his eyes running over the room.

She was seeing the same things he was. An open window. An untouched bed. The remains of a fire in the grate. Herbs scattered across the floor.

"It's the magic you were meddling with back in Jingen, isn't it?" Marielle asked, the realization bursting out of her before she thought about whether it was a good idea.

"I .. I .." he was stuttering, but he wasn't looking at her. His hands were running through his hair while he studied the room like he was reading his own death warrant. His mouth was open as if the answer were about to fall from it, but instead, all that poured from his parted lips were swirls of guilt mixed with fear. "I have to go after him."

Really? Still no answers? He was still going to leave her in the dark? Ignoring the splintered door, she grabbed his arm and dragged him to where the herbs were scattered on the ground. A tiny trail of smoke wove up from the ashes on the grate to the chimney above.

"Do you know what this is?" she asked him quietly. "Do you know what he did with this?"

"Yes," the words sounded like a confession, like she'd ripped them from his lips. She was going to get answers. Had he been in some kind of altered state when he rescued her? Was that it? Was it maybe not magic at all?

But it smelled like magic.

She steered him toward the bed and pushed him down into it so he was sitting on the edge and she could look him in the eyes. He was so tall. It was hard to be firm and intimidating when dealing with a man who was a head taller than she was.

"Are you able to perform magic like Etienne can sometimes?" she didn't want to mention the shell in her pocket or how she had access to magic now, too – even if she didn't really know how to use it.

"No," he breathed. His light-colored eyes were locked on hers, his expression so vulnerable as his scent deepened. The guilt in it – the aching anxiety of it – was growing in color and intensity with every heartbeat.

230

"But I smell it on you, just like I smelled it then." It was everywhere in this room – turquoise with golden sparkles. Vanilla and lilac licking at the edge of every thought like flames on the edge of a page. She wanted more of it. She wanted as much of it as she could get.

"I have a ... recipe ... to tap into things that go beyond what I can do," he said. "Did you read the page?"

She hadn't read it, though her eyes had brushed that one phrase, 'Bridge of Legends.' It stood out to her like a beacon in the night. After all, it was what Liandari was searching for. A way to bring back the Legends. She didn't want to admit how much she knew to Tamerlan. She needed to keep this to herself until she knew what the best thing to do with the information was. It felt like violating his trust not to share what she knew – but how far could she trust *him*?

She shook her head.

"Etienne has used it," he said and the look on his face was haunted. "And it's ... it's terribly dangerous."

"How dangerous?" she said, trying to stay calm. But the things Tamerlan had done in Jingen had been – awful. Horrific. Earth-shattering. They'd certainly destroyed everything she knew.

"Dangerous enough that the Butcher of the Temple District might seem tame compared to what could happen next. We need to find him, and we need to stop him before he destroys everything around him – like I did," Tamerlan said, fists clenched. He stood up suddenly and she had to step back.

"Maybe he won't," Marielle suggested. "The only thing Etienne has ever loved is his city. Maybe he just wants it back."

"Would he do anything for that, Marielle?" Tamerlan asked leaning in. She was uncomfortably aware of his strength and height as he loomed over her. He could snap her like a twig. Just like he'd snapped those poor partiers in the Temple District.

She shivered and then shrugged her answer.

"Would he destroy other cities? Other lives?" he pressed.

"He's a good man under everything," she said. But she wasn't certain. After all, Tamerlan seemed like a good man, too – sometimes. And the things he had done had stained him forever. "Maybe he can control it."

"It can't be controlled," Tamerlan said quietly. "It can only be contained."

He grabbed her wrists in his hands, but it didn't feel like he was trying to contain her. The look in his eyes was pleading and the spike in his emotions was a bright orange pulse of desperation.

"Please, Marielle." His eyes were wide and pleading. "Please help me hunt him down. Please help me stop him from making the same mistakes I did."

"How?" she asked. But, of course, she couldn't go with him. She needed to be here to help Anglarok and Liandari.

"Be my bloodhound. Follow his scent. I'll do whatever I have to do to keep us on his trail."

"He might not be far," Marielle said. Tamerlan was making it sound like they'd have to follow him for days over mountains and plains. Meanwhile, he might just be next door talking to Allegra.

There was something beautiful about Tamerlan's intensity. All his features went sharper as he spoke.

"I need you, Marielle. I need your help," His voice dropped to almost a whisper. "Please."

She swallowed, pulling her hands away. "Put some clothes on. You can't go chasing him while you're half- naked."

Tamerlan looked down, his face darkening as if he hadn't realized how little he was wearing.

She really shouldn't go. She still thought he was dangerous. She still owed more to the Harbingers. And yet – she could have prevented the massacre in the Temple District if she hadn't let Tamerlan go free that night. She could have prevented the fall of Jingen. She could have prevented everything if she'd just followed her own moral code instead of being persuaded to give him a chance.

Now, she was being asked again if she would try to stop disaster. She was being given a second chance. She didn't dare pass it up.

"Gather your things and meet me below in ten minutes," she said. "And be quiet. Liandari is hurt and we are not to wake her."

His excited expression was worrying, but the hungry scent flickering in the middle of his desperation was even worse. She was going to regret this.

# 28: Bloodhound

## *Tamerlan*

Tamerlan had been right about Etienne. He was not next door. He was not in the Spice District. Likely, he wasn't even in the city. But the route he'd taken was – unconventional.

Tamerlan had no sooner opened the door to the streets – still tightening his belt-pouch straps, slinging his jute bag over his shoulder, and hefting a small satchel Marielle had shoved at him – when she broke past him, nose forward, expression crisp and alert like the bloodhound he'd called her. She sprung from the steps of the inn, rushing into the crowd. Scarf swirling in the wind behind her.

"Wait!" he called, grabbing her arm.

She whirled, expression awash with irritation.

"I need to tell Jhinn where we are. He's waiting," Tamerlan said quickly. Despite her small size the intensity of her gaze made him step back.

"Hurry!" she barked, spinning again and stepping almost subconsciously forward.

He ran to where Jhinn had dropped them off along the canal. Hopefully, he was still there. If they were going to track Etienne, they were going to need a gondola.

"Jhinn!" he called before he'd even reached the canal. "Jhinn!"

He reached the railing, leaning down to see him there, standing in his gondola, craning his neck up to see Tamerlan. Tamerlan ducked under the rail and dropped down over the side of the wall and into the boat.

"You're in a hurry. You look almost as crazy as Etienne did," Jhinn commented with a yawn.

"You saw him? You saw Etienne?" Tamerlan gasped.

"You didn't tell me you were spreading those spirits around," he said.

And just like that, the Legends in Tamerlan's mind woke up again.

*Dragon. Dragon. Dragon.* Ram the Hunter.

*He stole your recipe! Now you've got some competition, pretty man!* Lila Cherrylocks.

*We will find him and bring him to justice. No nobles for us!* Byron Bronzebow.

The cruel cackling of Lady Chaos rang out behind them all and then a new voice stuttered to life.

*There's no treasure in this burned out hulk. Try north. Raiding inland cities can be fun if you know how they're fortified.* Deathless Pirate.

Now that he'd called a new Legend, he was stuck with him.

"Etienne had a spirit with him?" Tamerlan asked.

"He was possessed by one just like you. If you think I'm gonna smoke that stuff, you can think again. I kept your stash, and I rolled more for you, and I lied to Etienne and told him I knew nothing about any of that, and told him to hire someone else to take him upriver, but I'm not calling any spirits myself. That's your job."

Tamerlan's heart was in his throat as he asked, "What spirit did you see with him?"

"Possessing him, you mean? Grandfather Timeless. And trust me, he's not a nice grandfather. A cruel old man is more accurate."

Dragon's spit in a cup! He'd been taken over by Grandfather Timeless? But how long could that last? One smoking would only last a few hours.

"He had herbs with him," Jhinn said. "I don't know if they'll be enough, but they were stuffed into a satchel and I could see the edges of some of the leaves sticking out."

"Can you follow us through the city? I'm tracking where he went with Marielle, but his path might not go along the canals."

"Shouldn't we just go to the river? That's the way out of the city."

"But on which side? I don't know where he's headed. But I would guess it's somewhere out of town."

"I would guess it's wherever the Grandfather wants to take him."

Tamerlan nodded briskly. He needed to get back to Marielle before she tore through the city without him.

"Here," Jhinn said, grabbing his bags and tossing them into the boat and then shoving a small whistle into his hand. "Blow this every few minutes and I'll hear it and stay close in the canals."

Tamerlan grinned. "You're a good friend, Jhinn."

"Don't tell anyone. I have a reputation to uphold!"

Tamerlan blew the whistle, and then, with a laugh, he hopped onto the lip of the canal and ran to the nearest staircase and back up into the street.

Where was Marielle? Not where he'd left her, and no surprise there.

He blew the whistle when he reached the point where he'd asked her to stay and then he ran on, glancing up each alley and side street until he finally found her hopping up and down on her toes at a crossroads.

"Come on!" she said, grabbing his arm the second she saw him and surging through the growing crowd.

"Best honey wafers! Break your fast this fine Dawnspell!" one vendor was crying as they passed his red cart, their feet flying across the cobbles.

"He went this way," Marielle said, weaving between a man pushing a barrow of lumber and a woman wheeling a cart of honey in jars.

"Watch it!" the man with the timber said. "We need this to rebuild my shop! Dragon take you if I spill the load!"

"As if timber is more important than honey on Dawnspell!" the woman argued, her red face growing redder. "There is no Xin without the holidays. No shop at all without customers and the ceremonies keep us from the judgment of the Legends!"

"Ha! Tell that to my wife!"

But their voices were already fading as Tamerlan blew the whistle beside a canal railing and then Marielle gripped his arm, dragging him down a lonely side street and emerging on the other side near to where the cliffs rose up into the Government District.

Tamerlan felt worry crawl in his belly. What if Lord Mythos wasn't leaving town at all? What if his plans involved the palace here and Tamerlan's sister? He swallowed down rising bile. The thought of the Lord Mythos near his sister again brought back too many memories. He looked down at his hands and the memory of them bathed bright in blood made him shudder.

He blew the whistle, hoping Jhinn could hear from so far away, but they were already ascending the stairs up, up, up the white cliffs between the Districts.

"This way," Marielle said. Her eyes were bright with the hunt. Every muscle tense, every sense employed. She was beautiful as a hunting bird, as a falcon, as a hawk wheeling in the air. He imagined her in another life, soaring on wings with perfect feathers, bucking the updrafts, diving in wide arcs, hunting by sight and scent until her prey was cornered and helpless. As he had been when she'd let him go. As Etienne would be when he was found.

"Tamerlan?" her question interrupted him, and he shook himself. He'd paused as the daydream swallowed him. There was no time for that. None of the Legends were safe and one on the loose wasn't something to wink at. Not even Grandfather Timeless.

*Grandfather Timeless is the most dangerous Legend to be loose! He has plans. And this is his festival.*

"Sorry," he said with a half-smile and Marielle nodded sharply, pulling him through the crowds. "Can you smell which – I mean, can you smell if he's set one of the Legends free?"

He grabbed her by the arms, pulling her from the path of a rumbling cart at the last second. Her eyes never left her trail. Tamerlan could have traced it with chalk even though he couldn't see it himself, just by following her gaze.

"I can smell magic. That's all. And him. I can smell him."

A pang of jealousy flashed across his heart at the thought of her doing something so intimate as drawing Etienne's scent into her lungs. Now, why would that bother him so much?

Why should he feel jealousy over something he didn't own and never could?

She stepped out across a surge of people and Tamerlan forced his way forward, using his body to block the crowd from bowling her over. She really wasn't watching anything except for the scent!

"I think he's possessed by Grandfather Timeless," he said as she led him out of the heavier crowds to a small walkway between buildings. A last elbow struck him in the ribs, and he breathed a sigh of relief as they cleared the crowds. Honeysuckle hung heavily on arches over the path and she seemed momentarily distracted by the scent of it before she continued on her path. "It is said that Grandfather Timeless wrote all our lives in time already, before they were ever lived or even conceived of. He chronicled every daydream, every idle thought, every shattered hope."

She glanced back at him, a mixture of curiosity and revulsion in her expression. Why revulsion?

*Girls don't like men making decisions for them,* Lila Cherrylocks offered.

"Then why live life at all?" Marielle asked. "If it's already been written?"

"Because the joy is in the living," Tamerlan said simply.

"Joy for who?" Marielle asked as they emerged where a canal ran alongside the Government District.

241

Tamerlan blew his whistle and then looked down at her. "Well, that's the big question, isn't it?"

He winked, but she just shook her head as if he was exasperating her. Didn't she like thinking about life's big questions?

*Not when she's trying to get something done.*

Jhinn's little gondola emerged a moment later and he waved to them with a smile.

"Is that what the whistle is for?" Marielle asked, surprise in her face.

"How else would he find us?"

"Good," she said, her expression sharp, her tone all business. "I think he left town through a back way at the rear of the Government District. I smell water and brass there. I suspect there are locks for the gondola. Let's go."

"Still on the trail?" Jhinn asked as Tamerlan and Marielle stepped from the canal step to the gondola he'd just pulled up alongside them.

Marielle scrambled to the front of the boat, sitting on top of the smooth wood that covered the forward compartment.

"This way," she said, pointing ahead.

Tamerlan boarded a bit more carefully. He'd worn everything that Etienne had provided for him – including metal armor. One false move and the gondola could capsize, and he would sink to the bottom.

He settled himself carefully on the seat.

"Lose the metal," Jhinn said wryly. "And get ready to row. I have a bad feeling that he's well ahead of you by now."

# 29: Sealed in Prisons

*TAMERLAN*

"I've lost the scent. It smells like it's hours old, but that just doesn't make sense!" Marielle said, her voice wavering as they reached the bottom of the locks and shot out past the wharves and into the river.

This branch of the Cerulean – known as the North Branch – was rough. A wind was rising, blowing from inland and bringing the scents of growing things and fecund earth.

Marielle stood, holding the ferro and leaning out over a new lantern – when had Jhinn found time to replace that? – and scenting the wind. Her face was screwed up in a mixture of perplexity and frustration.

"It was here a moment ago and now it smells hours old. That makes no sense!"

*Makes perfect sense. Grandfather Timeless controls time. I feel like I shouldn't have to say that.*

Lila Cherrylocks must have been insufferable when she was alive.

*I didn't spend much time with idiots, so it wasn't a problem. Clearly, he's bending time to his will. You're lagging pretty far behind. This would be a good time to open the Bridge and catch up!*

Of course, she would say that. She was just itching to get out. But what good would having Lila Cherrylocks be in a boat? She couldn't row any faster with his arms than he could, and she couldn't bend time.

*Don't look a gift horse in the mouth! You'd be surprised at the kind of things I can do.*

Uh huh. Like going off on her own quest and completely forgetting what he was after? No. Tamerlan had learned his lesson. He couldn't rely on the Legends and he wouldn't try.

His resolve began to fail after the first few hours in the beating sun.

Marielle had slumped in the bottom of the boat, worn out from trying to smell a scent long cold, while Jhinn and Tamerlan rowed against a hard wind, bucking against the waves battling against them one after another. Even on a good day, it would be difficult travel, but with their current frustration and discouragement, it was worse. It wore at them until Marielle fell asleep. Jhinn and Tamerlan fought the waves in silence. The wind was too loud to hear each other speak and they were too frustrated to have anything encouraging to say.

It was well past noon when they found the hulk of a family boat floating in the river and a few minutes later when they found the boat that had saved them, both families huddled against the harsh wind.

"Your boat looks like it burned," Jhinn called over the wind. "Mer send you all were saved!"

"Mer had nothing to do with it!" one of the women on the boat said, shaking an angry middle-aged fist at the sky. "It was a man dressed in black. He demanded to know what time it was and when we told him, he lit our boat on fire! He said it was 'too late.' As if we have any control over the time of day! We lost everything! Everything."

Her husband patted her on the shoulder, his own eyes hollow and worn and as Jhinn exchanged consolations with them, Tamerlan felt his blood running cold. He shook Marielle awake.

"Do you smell him now?"

She woke to immediate sharpness, scrambling to her feet and thrusting her nose forward.

"He was here," she confirmed. He's all over this place. It's fresh. Only a few hours old."

Jhinn said his goodbyes, and Tamerlan spoke condolences, but Marielle's eyes were fixed on the horizon as they pulled back into the river.

"Just up ahead," she called over the wind.

Tamerlan felt his mouth go dry. They were not far behind. In this wind, Jhinn's fleet craft and two men rowing just had to be enough to overtake the Lord Mythos, possessed or not.

But when they reached the next bend of the river, Marielle was shaking her head again.

"I don't understand it. It's like he's here one minute and then gone the next! The trail has vanished. It smells days old!"

Tamerlan patted her arm.

"It's okay," he said. "Maybe we'll find it again."

But as she slumped again, discouraged, he felt his own mind racing. What would happen if you had a Legend possessing you who could hop through time? Could you go back and fix mistakes from the past?

*Unlikely,* Byron Bronzebow said sharply. *Things that happened tend to stay happened.*

But Etienne was hopping and jumping in time. So why wasn't he headed to Jingen to fix their mistakes and restore the city? That's what Tamerlan would do if he was given the chance and he could have sworn that Etienne felt the same way. Of course, if anyone knew how fickle the Legends could be, it was Tamerlan. Maybe Etienne wasn't getting what he wanted from the Legend any more than Tamerlan usually did.

*A Legend inhabiting a person through the Bridge of Legends is not a powerful enough connection to do so great a Feat as restoring a city.*

Lila pronounced 'feat' like it had a capital letter – like it meant something akin to 'Legend.'

*Legends produce Feats. They are our great acts. Like when I stole the Abercauler Crown. Or when Abelmeyer used his Eye to chain the city dragons. They are our great acts that define our lives and generation. To*

247

*step back and restore an entire city? That would be a Feat. And to do that, a Legend would have to walk in the flesh.*

"But that's impossible," Tamerlan said.

*Is it? You saw Deathless Pirate's avatar trapped in the cage, didn't you?*

At the mention of his name the pirate roared in Tamerlan's mind. *Trapped! Trapped under the briny sea!*

He was going to go mad with all these voices in his head.

*Grandfather Timeless has an avatar, too. We all do. They were sealed up by Queen Mer's people. Trapped in objects or prisons. But if Grandfather Timeless's avatar was free, then who knows what he could do.*

Perhaps he could turn back time. Perhaps he could undo mistakes.

*I'm telling you,* Byron insisted. *Things done, stay done. It's madness to think otherwise.*

"I'm not mad," Tamerlan said aloud.

"But you sure sound like you are when you talk to yourself like that," Jhinn said.

Tamerlan shook himself, swallowing down a curse. Marielle was asleep in the bottom of the boat again. All this scenting was wearing her out. Only Jhinn had seen his slip.

"Did I say that out loud?" he asked.

"Sure. Not that listening to the spirits talk to you isn't entertaining, but do you think you should encourage them like that?" Jhinn asked. "I think madness will follow you if you walk that road."

He was right. Tamerlan needed to solve this conundrum without the Legends.

*You need us.* Lila insisted.

*Dragon. Dragon. Dragon.*

And encouraging them wasn't helping.

With effort, he forced them from his mind.

They found a restaurant barge just before dark, and though it would only sell honey cakes and wafers on Dawnspell, they loaded up on them and ate. Tamerlan let the sweetness of the honeycakes fill him as Jhinn looked for a good spot to tie the boat along the edge of the river.

"We can't make H'yi tonight – if that's where he's going. The scent is cold. The night is falling. Our best bet is to wait here," Jhinn said practically as the gondola slid through reeds as tall as they were. "We can eat. We can rest. Maybe in the morning, we will find something new."

Tamerlan nodded tiredly.

"Unless you want to try another way?" Jhinn let the words hang in the air, his gaze resting on the small leather pouch he'd given Tamerlan earlier in the day. It contained more of his mixture rolled in paper – at least thirty little paper sticks of it. He could be possessed by a Legend every night for a month with those! He'd tried to hand the bag back, but Jhinn had insisted.

"It's yours," he'd said. "I just rolled them up to pass the time."

"I think rest is a good idea," Tamerlan said firmly.

Jhinn was already dragging blankets out of his waterproof boat trailer when Marielle spoke into the night.

"I shouldn't have left them. They needed me and I just went running off like a puppy with a fresh scent."

"The Harbingers?" Tamerlan guessed. "They'll be fine. They're fierce warriors. Besides, if Etienne is up to what I think he's up to, then you'll be glad that you took the chance to stop him."

"Why do I keep losing his scent?" she muttered as if to herself.

"Because he has tricks up his sleeve that we can't even imagine," Tamerlan said. "We'll pick it up again. This can't last forever."

It was amazing it had lasted this long, honestly. After all, he'd only had one good fire with his recipe. They only ever lasted a few hours for Tamerlan.

Except, the recipe didn't have quantities. Tamerlan had just followed his instinct when he combined the ingredients. How had Etienne mixed the ingredients? Tamerlan hadn't stopped to ask that question. He hadn't asked how the other man made the formula. The man who had scrawled on the page had failed. And Tamerlan had assumed that when he tried, he'd only succeeded as a matter of lucking out. But what if Etienne had the same luck – but better? What if he'd stumbled on a more potent formula for the recipe? What if he was … better than Tamerlan?

Tamerlan swallowed, hoping he was wrong. Hoping he was just being paranoid, but as they settled in for sleep in the rocking boat against the river bank, he found it hard to rest. Somewhere out there, someone smarter than him was using his magic. And he'd learned the hard way that being intelligent was no shield at all against evil. On the contrary, it seemed to only amplify the destruction that could be caused.

# 30: In the Dark of Night

*MARIELLE*

The magic had been too powerful. All day, the power of it had assaulted her mind, laying her out on the bottom of the boat sometimes, so that her companions thought she was sleeping when in fact she was struggling to clear her migraine for long enough to be able to smell again.

When the trail was cold it wasn't so bad – then she only smelled the residue on Tamerlan, but the golden scent of her overpowering attraction to him made the scent of magic so much worse so that every vibration of his voice sent thrills through her like electric shocks. Every casual glance of his in her direction left little shivers pulsing through her. Her own response only amplified the scent so that it spun ever upward in a spiral lifting to the heavens even while she was sure it was actually plunging her toward hell.

She knew what he was. By the admission of his own lips – his own curving, half-smiling lips – he was guilty of the blood of innocents. Anything that drew her closer to him could only break her heart – and yet she was still drawn. Breath by breath, moment by moment she was drawn. The close confines of the boat made it worse. The way he kept watching her as if he were admiring the way she could Scent made it worse. The way Jhinn smirked when he caught her looking at Tamerlan made it worse. Everything made it worse.

And when they hit those pockets of scent – those moments when she could smell Etienne swirling in the madness of magic and something else – something older than the dragon and just as powerful – something that wanted to eat her alive. When she smelled those, then the pain that filled her head was almost more than she could take, but her lungs wouldn't stop gulping the magic in, breath after breath until her head was light and she felt as if she might faint.

Twice she'd had to slump to the bottom of the boat, recovering as her head swirled with magic. But her ears still worked even if she appeared to be asleep. She'd hear Tamerlan's mad ranting and Jhinn's talk of spirits. And she felt nervous about that.

And even more nervous as the tattoo over her heart throbbed stronger and stronger the further she went from Liandari and Anglarok. She shouldn't have left them without word of where she was going. She shouldn't have kept Anglarok in the dark. She should have come clean to them about what she'd seen on that illuminated page. Perhaps, if they were searching for the Bridge of Legends then they might know how to stop this flood of evil spirits entering the world. After all, it was why they were here.

She huddled in her corner of the boat and tried to sleep as the velvet darkness closed in around the gondola. Jhinn had lit the lamp hanging from the ferro at the front of the gondola, but around the tiny pool of light lurked darkness on every side. The bobbing lights of glowbugs in the distance, the soothing calls of birds back and forth, the chatter of frogs, and the chirping of insects were not enough to set her at ease. Not even when her Scenting told her there was nothing nearby in any direction except for river and mud and natural creatures.

She sucked in a deep breath and tried to sleep, curling into her blankets. Tried to ignore the scent of Jhinn – familiar and easy. Tried to ignore the scent of Tamerlan – overwhelmingly tempting, especially now as the sweat of his hard work dried in the balmy warm wind, drawing up his physical musk and stirring it into the golden scent of attraction. He was forbidden fruit. The one apple in the orchard no human should touch. The one sword that if drawn from the stone would ignite a war to kill them all. So why did he smell so delectable?

She reached into her belt pouch, reminding herself that the small conch shell was still there. Her link to sanity. Her link to another way, if she could just keep reaching for it instead of giving into temptation.

She must have fallen asleep drinking in that forbidden scent because she woke to rough fabric wrapping around her face. She tried to scream, but a hand clamped tightly over her mouth and nose. She couldn't breathe, couldn't smell who was attacking her. She tried to gasp in a breath, but the hand was too strong. Worse, there was something on it – or on a rag it was holding – something that smelled suspiciously like aniseed oil. Her eyes teared up and her head began to whirl as she began to slip away from consciousness. She felt her body being lifted up and carried, but she heard nothing. No sound to alert her friends to what had happened. No tell-tale cry of someone waking in the night to enemies. Nothing.

Her head spun from lack of oxygen and the overpowering scent and she balled her fists, fighting against her attacker, but her punches were weak, her strength fading. Suddenly, the hand shifted, covering only her mouth and she sucked in a deep breath through dank wool. It wasn't helping. It wasn't clearing her mind fast enough.

Through the smell of aniseed she thought she might b smelling Etienne – mandarin oranges and cloves. But it was tangled up in the fierce turquoise and gold of magic and ... something else and so much aniseed that she wanted to be sick. And the voice that whispered to her wasn't Etienne's at all.

"Sleep, little child. For this night is written as the night of your capture and the beginning of your doom."

Her heart was in overdrive. He must be joking if he thought she would sleep! She would fight until the oxygen stole from her lungs. A fresh cloth was applied to her nose – a larger does than before. Her thoughts faded as she spun to blackness.

She woke to inky darkness.

Woke to wind whipping around her as she jostled step after step in the most awkward position. Her hands and feet were bound and she was slung over someone's back, her legs tied tightly around his waist. His hip bones dug into her thighs with every step and his bony shoulder blade crashed into her cheek. There was a glow that barely lit the grass around them.

"Awake little child? I sent you back into your sleep and then we leapt forward here. I can't jump far, but I can still jump a little and this body is fine and fit."

She hated the wheedling high-pitched tone that wavered in the middle of sentences, like an old man trying to be cunning but forgetting what the secret was that he was supposed to keep hidden.

"Did we walk all night?" she asked, as he strode through river reeds. They stroked her hanging hair and slipped across her smooth cheeks with a *whish whish* sound.

"Not yet. Time is running out. We must hurry. The boat is lost, but the will stays strong!"

Then it was almost Spellbreak. The last day of Dawnspell. If only this spell could be broken and whatever had seized Etienne could be forced to let him go. If only she could escape his clutches somehow.

"What do you want with me?" she asked boldly.

"Your blood, little child."

She shuddered. It always came back to blood.

"Any Dragonblooded will do, but you are the one he knows about. And you weren't far away. That makes you perfect. We won't take it all. Just a drop. Just a drop. It's only as a back up in case the plan doesn't work."

"That's what they all say," Marielle said bitterly. "'It's only as a back up,' they say and then they chain you to feed a dragon."

He laughed a horrible wheezing laugh like a man on his last legs – not at all like Etienne. "We won't be feeding any dragons today. But yes, your life might be required. It usually is."

She could smell his certainty. And she could smell that there was no pity mixed in it. No regret. No hope for her at all.

"Oh, don't sulk. Some lives are worth less than others. I've seen yours written out and it's not all that spectacular. You won't be missing much. In fact, you might even thank me because I'll give you something in return."

"Oh yeah? Are you going to give me *your* life?"

This time his wheezing laugh was so deep it bent him double. "I almost like you."

His scent said otherwise. He was just as indifferent toward her as he'd been before she spoke

"But no, I'll be keeping my life. Enough of that has been stolen already. Yes, I'll be keeping that. But I'll give you my immortality."

"Just like that?"

This time the wheezing went on and on and on.

"You say that like you think it's a gift," he choked out eventually. "Instead of the curse it really is. Wait until you've stood frozen in a clock for a thousand years, conscious, thinking, but frozen in place. So bored you would chew through your own mind just to be free, like a trapped animal will chew off its own leg. Just wait for that. Then you can thank me for your immortality."

"I'd ask you to put me down, but why make your job easier?" Marielle said.

"I'd ask you to stop with the barbed comments," he wheezed, "but then how would I have my fun?"

Marielle gritted her teeth as they trudged on. Already the hours seemed endless, and she wasn't even stuck in a clock yet. She wondered if Etienne had any power at all under the grip of this spirit – Grandfather Timeless, if Tamerlan was right – or if he was as helpless as she was in the thrall of this horrific Legend.

# 31: DESPERATE TIMES

## *TAMERLAN*

Tamerlan's dreams had been nothing but nightmares. He'd tossed and sweated through dreams of Marielle in trouble. The last dream had been the worst. He'd been too late in the Grand Hall and they'd slit her throat right in front of him. As her scarlet blood fountained onto the scales of the dragon his own sister had laughed, clapping her hands in delight.

Tamerlan woke with his hands balled in fists, his teeth on edge. But it hadn't happened that way. Others had died while he'd saved her life. The dream made it all feel so fresh – like he was reliving it again. And this time with a different decision. But choosing the other option didn't make him feel less guilty. It didn't still the angry voices in his head. He woke to dry lips and aching muscles and a strange dull orange glow in the sky. And then silence.

He sat up.

Marielle's place in the boat was empty, her blanket gone. Orange light danced across the empty place where she should be sleeping. He looked to Jhinn. The other boy was wide-eyed as he struggled to sit up. He licked his lips nervously.

"You didn't hear her leave?" he asked.

"No," Tamerlan breathed.

"She had no reason to go on her own?"

"No," Tamerlan agreed. But without her, they had no Scenter, and no way to track her or anyone else. "She must have been taken."

But who would have taken her?

*Grandfather Timeless can have an interesting perspective on morality,* Lila said in his mind.

A thief thought that his morality wasn't up to snuff?

*It's easy to mistake writing people's fates for being the one with the authority to change their fates. We used to have names for him. The Grandfather. The Fatemaker.*

He sounded charming. But where would he be taking Marielle?

*To the clock. To his avatar.*

"Are you worried about that light?" Jhinn asked mildly, pointing to the orange glow in the sky to the north.

"It looks like a big fire. Like a city burning," Tamerlan said, running his hand through his hair. What now? How could he track Grandfather Timeless and Marielle without her ability to Scent and with Jhinn confined to the boat?

"I think it's H'yi. The glow is in the right direction." Jhinn coughed. "I hate to say this."

Tamerlan watched a smirk form on his friend's face in the faint glow of the distant fire.

"Somehow, I doubt that."

"You need to smoke your stuff. You need to call the spirits to help. We aren't far from the city but with it on fire and our Scenter gone, it's the only chance of catching up."

Tamerlan gritted his teeth. "I said I'd never do that again."

"And yet, you did it to steal the amulet."

"In a controlled environment! When I knew you could shut things down if they got out of hand!"

Jhinn laughed. "Yeah. Like I could have beaten that Pirate spirit if he attacked me. No. Not even with the sword. But you came out of that unscathed." He paused. "Except for the part where you nearly drowned."

Tamerlan cleared his throat. Why did it feel like there was a ball lodged in it?

"Come on. Just a little bit," Jhinn urged. "Keep the roll up in your hand and refresh it when you need to."

"I won't do that. I won't be able to get my own body back."

"Okay, then keep the pouch of them handy. If you run out of spirit, just smoke again and you'll be back. I don't think you're going to have trouble finding a fire to light it with."

Tamerlan nodded. They were already settling at the oars and pushing off. He shivered in the night as they sped into the darkness, the bobbing light of the lantern on the ferro lighting the way.

"Do you think the dragon is back?" Jhinn asked, just as a gust of wind rocked their gondola to the side.

A shadow crossed the moon. It was the shape of a dragon.

They rowed harder.

They hadn't rowed far when the first boats came into view, heading downriver with the current.

"Turn around," the boatman called from a family boat racing by. "Save yourselves before it's too late!"

A moment later a barge passed.

"You're going the wrong way!" the barge master shouted. "Turn around."

And then they were weaving through a steady stream of boats – family boats stuffed with tired people calling out to them to flee, barges laden with goods or wild-eyed people, even gondolas packed with passengers and all of them calling to them.

"Flee while you can! The city burns! H'yi burns!"

At the next bend in the river, it was obvious why. Smoke wreathed H'yi – glowing orange in the night as flames leapt up. Anyone could be forgiven for thinking the whole city was ablaze. But as Tamerlan peered into the smoke, he thought that it was only a few buildings right now – some of the larger ones, certainly, but only about a half-dozen.

"Drop me off on the bank and I'll go the rest of the way myself," he called to Jhinn.

"Ha! Let's not play this game again," Jhinn said, rowing harder. "You know I love the adventure and you're not leaving me behind!"

"It looks like hell in there," Tamerlan called through gritted teeth. It was becoming more difficult to weave through the boats on the glutted river. Every craft in the city was fleeing.

"I've told you before that everything out of the water is the land of the Satan. This time you see it burning, next time you'll think it is safe, but to me, it is always deathly dangerous."

How did you tell a friend to stop being so selfless in a way he would obey? He was going to have to think up a better way for next time.

Smoke and char puffed in irregular clouds across the water as they reached the city. They had passed the last boat a moment ago – a rotting hulk that was only barely floating. But any boat was safety right now and anyone who owned one was fleeing in it. The canals ahead of them were shockingly empty. And above them, noise filled the city as people fought the fires sweeping across their city. Hopefully, more had fled by land.

Tamerlan scanned the sky, but it was still too dark to make out the dragon unless he crossed the moon. Up there somewhere, Jingen soared through the darkness, reveling in the chaos and terror below. Up there somewhere, the dragon was plotting revenge for a thousand years of captivity.

Tamerlan felt tension growing in his belly when they hit the first set of locks. There was no one manning them. No way for them to climb through the city via canal.

Jhinn cursed, maneuvering the boat to where the chains and hydraulics were located in a little cabin beside the canal.

"Go in there and raise the water level," he said.

"How?" Tamerlan asked.

Jhinn shrugged.

"Right. Land of the Satan. That's my territory, right?" Tamerlan asked, but he leapt out and ran into the cabin immediately.

Fortunately, the locks were made to be operated by people happy to sit and watch a canal all day. They were simple to operate and after a single false start, the water rose up to the next level.

Tamerlan leapt from the canal edge into the gondola as Jhinn sped onward.

"Which way?" Jhinn asked.

"I think the clock is in the Government District," he said.

*Think again. Who in this city worships clocks?*

And as if drawn by Lila's words, the bells of the city began to ring the hour. Three o'clock.

"Scratch that. Go to the Temple District," Tamerlan said. If the Timekeepers worshiped Time, it stood to reason that they would have the clock with his avatar.

*Precisely.*

*Dragon. Dragon. Dragon.*

Ram was growing louder as they passed the first burning building, a tall smokehouse in the Spice District. Just like in Xin. The dragon certainly had a favorite target. Tamerlan shivered as he watched buckets of water thrown at the spiraling flames as if that could possibly do anything to stop their rampage. Already, the roofs on either side of the smokehouse were wreathed in flame.

He leaned over his oars and rowed, the heat of the fires searing his skin as they passed. Steam rose up off the canal in steady swirls and the gondola hissed as the wood dried in the intense heat. They were past the fire in moments, but each moment had felt like an eternity. Already, Tamerlan was slick with sweat as he fought the oars, leaping into the little cabin the moment he saw it at the next lock.

They rose up to the Temple District, flying down the canal. Above them, long lines of Timekeepers strode down the street above them, holding bells.

"What are they doing?" Jhinn called out as they passed the white-cloaked worshippers.

"Spellend," Tamerlan said. "On Spellend the Timekeepers wake up at the first hour and parade through the streets ringing bells until dawn when everyone bathes in cold water to signify the end of Dawnspell and the washing of the past to start new. Surely, you must have seen that in Jingen."

"Yes, but usually not when there's a raging fire right in their district!" Jhinn pointed down the canal to where the tallest temple – a Timekeeper Cathedral burned. Only the tower was on fire – right now. The tallest spire flickered as the flame spread. How long would it take a building like that to burn? And where was this clock he was looking for?

*In front of that cathedral. That's the Cathedral of the Clock.*

Tamerlan felt his mouth go dry.

# 32: CATHEDRAL OF THE CLOCK

*MARIELLE*

If the city hadn't been in chaos when they arrived, someone might have noticed a woman being carried on a man's back. They would have noticed that her hands and feet were tied. They would have noticed she was fighting as hard as she could to get free.

If the city hadn't been burning, then the Watch would have stopped Etienne – or Grandfather Timeless – or whoever this was who was carrying her through the night into the glorious city of H'yi. If the guards at the gates hadn't been watching the sky, crossbows trained on the night, watching for the flicker of moonlight on scale, then they would have stopped them and asked questions. If the shoals of terrified people weren't pushing out of the city like a surge of loose farm animals, desperate to escape the sound of their own slaughter, then someone would have at least noticed.

But no one did.

267

She coughed and choked on gouts of smoke, fighting against her captor. She couldn't choke him – not with her arms pulled so far forward and held in place by one of his hands. More than once, he cuffed her in the head to make her stop fighting, but she wouldn't stop. No one grabbed girls and tied them up for good reasons. No one was ever tied up and then brought to a cheery room full of fresh fruit and a door opening to wide fields or a secluded forest and told, 'Just enjoy yourself and leave when you want.' That didn't happen.

What did happen to girls who were grabbed and tied up was more like what she and Carnelian had found on her first patrol. Marielle had smelled what was below before they even broke down the doors in the fish market. She'd been on the side spilling her breakfast all over the street long before they dragged the bodies out of the hull of the barge that had been stowed under the fish smokers. But that hadn't stopped her from dry heaving when Carnelian told her that some of those girls were still alive.

She'd vowed right then that she'd never be taken alive. Better to die fighting than live to watch yourself die in some worse way. It was the waiting that she thought would be the worst part – the endless waiting knowing that death was your only way out. And yet, here she was, still alive despite fighting so hard.

"Fight all you want," that horrible high-pitched voice whispered to her. "It will only tire you. And I want you tired for what comes next."

Her belly lurched at his words, but she fought harder, biting his shoulder with her teeth until she tasted blood and thought he must be leaving a trail of it behind him. It didn't even slow him.

She heard bells ringing the fifth hour of the night as they pressed through thick bodies and the swishing of robes. She smelled the Temple District. The smoke of the Smudgers – mostly sage but with other additions – still hung in the air long after the practitioners had left and mixed with the dust and bronze of the Timekeepers. Religious sanctimony and a thick band of deceit colored the snatches of cobblestones and robes that she saw. She'd heard that the Timekeepers always wore white, but to her eyes, they wore pride like a violet robe and deceit like a greeny-yellow scarf. She almost gagged on the thick emotions of this place. At the height of Dawnspell when all of the rest of the Dragonblood Plains were cleansing themselves, the Temple District stank like midden with rotten power and misused souls.

She gagged and her captor hurried his steps.

Smoke tinged the air – just buildings so far. No humans. Not yet. But if the heat she felt – the heat slicking her body in sweat and making her mouth dry as paper – was anything to judge by, then soon the fires would be worse, and then people would die.

Anyone with sense should be fleeing the city, not forcing their way to the heart of it. Not ringing their bells like mindless drones in love with their own magnificence more than life.

Her captor fumbled with something and then her legs were free, hanging down, frozen with the stiffness of being immobilized for so long. He spun her around to the front of him, her arms still bound around her neck. She clenched her jaw, willing life into her legs. This was her chance to get free. He'd know she was hampered by pain and frozen limbs and think she was helpless. She could take advantage of that.

Her fate looked at her with grim analysis from only inches away as she stomped her feet, trying to bring back feeling. Oddly, the expression suited Etienne. Even taken over by this spirit, the sharp look was in his eyes and the careful tactical judgment he always exercised painted his expression. His emotions were a terrible tangle. On the one hand, there was a surge of ambition and exultation. On the other hand, a squirming discomfort and shame – as if he were two men in one, fighting for the tiller of his soul.

"The city is in flames," she said. "Whatever you are trying to do can't take precedence over the dragon. He needs to be stopped."

Etienne laughed and the laugh sounded nothing like him – as if he were opening his mouth while someone else stood behind him and made the sound.

"Tamerlan said you stole Abelmeyer's Eye," Marielle said. "Can't you use it to stop the dragon?"

Etienne leaned in, the huge ruby around his neck slipping out of his shirt for a moment before he tucked it back in. He was close to her height and it was surprising that his wiry frame had carried her so far and so quickly – as if the strength from within was overriding all his body's limits.

"Who says I want to stop it?" he asked, his eyes glittering in the glow of firelight.

He lifted her arms, slipping his head out from between them.

She didn't hesitate. She began to run the second his head was out from between her arms. She was awkward with her hands tied, but she shoved every ounce of energy into her strides. She barely made it four steps before something tangled in her long hair, wrenching her backward. She cried out, fighting against the hand, but it buried deeper, yanking her neck sharply to one side and then forcing her in front of him.

She dropped to her knees. She wouldn't make this easy for him.

"I don't need you to walk. It's not *my* pretty hair that will be torn out by the roots."

He strode forward, dragging her by her hair as she screamed. She shoved her bound hands forward and managed to flip back up onto her feet, stumbling to keep up as he forced her up a long, shallow flight of marble stairs.

"The Cathedral of the Clock!" a man gasped as he flew by. "We're going to lose it!"

Feet few up and down the steps as people rushed with buckets in hand and soot smeared across their faces and clothing. Droplets of water flew from the edges of the water-soaked rags that clung to their faces, framing their desperate eyes. For once in her life, Marielle was not the one with her face wrapped against the onslaught.

"It's aflame! The dragon set it on fire!"

"Oh, sweet Legends!" a voice gasped.

"The history of H'yi!" another moaned. "The glory of our people!"

None of them noticed Marielle being forced to her knees as they reached the top of the steps before the looming white Cathedral of the Clock. She knew this place immediately. Would have known it from the description alone even if she hadn't heard the worried cries.

Marielle craned her neck to look upward past the soaring face of the cathedral, the carefully set glass panels of the stained glass, the domed roof swirling with flame and the spire sticking up from the top like the stamen from a crimson flower. Ashes as wide as her palm, still cherry red, drifted down from the sky.

"Wha … wha … wha …" she tried to say, but it came out as stuttering because through the crowd she smelled overpowering magic laced with so much fear and horror that she couldn't seem to think. Terror swirled in the air in wide, raw, red ribbons as fear crackled along the edges and shattered her nose with vinegar and acid.

"My worshippers," Grandfather Timeless said with delight, forcing her forward to the front of the cathedral where before the entrance stood a soaring grandfather clock. Its base was rooted here in front of the wide double doors of the cathedral, a pendulum there – but not there – flickering with ghostly blue light and then back to a frizzling smoke as it swung ponderously back and forth behind the glass.

The clock was not on fire like everything else. It was almost as if it wasn't entirely in this world. As if it couldn't catch fire.

Marielle shivered, remembering the bonging domed clock at the Seven Suns Palace. It had spelled her doom. But this one – this one felt worse.

Gleaming in white marble, the clock soared toward the sky. Its face and moondial were wrought of stained glass and stood as high as the peak of the cathedral. It's finials and planton nearly reached to the top of the cathedral's dome.

"The Clock of Ages," Grandfather Timeless said and in his mouth, it sounded like a curse.

The marble of the case was intricately carved with the protective wings of angels and the flowers of a hundred gardens but weaving between the flowers and wings was black wrought iron that looked horrifically like a cage. It crackled and popped with electric turquoise and the smell of magic was so strong around it that Marielle swayed under the power of it.

There – but not there at the same time – through the glass of the lower door, a ghostly figure flicked in and out of life whenever the pendulum crossed its silhouette. Crackling sparks and flowing blue power sparked at that point before the figure faded again from view. He appeared to be frozen – stuck in one terrible pose with a single hand lifted pleadingly for all of time.

It was a surreal object – so heavenly – and yet not. And with the fires swirling behind it as worshipful Timekeepers in flowing robes rushed to douse the flames, it looked for all the world like a space between heaven and hell.

Marielle never wanted to hear another clock.

Never.

At least this one wasn't spelling out her doom.

"How many seconds are there in a thousand years, Marielle?" Etienne purred in her ear. His voice was smooth, but his emotions were a tangle of frantic excitement and desperate terror. Behind the clock, there was a loud crack as part of the dome of the Cathedral of the Clock caved in. "How many fractions of a second? I feel every one. I experience every single one. In stasis. I know the end of every story, the lie behind every truth. Nothing can surprise me. There is no joy left undiscovered, no brighter future tomorrow, no blessed sleep to clear the mind. No forgetfulness to mend the shattered heart. There is only the long, slow, infinite march of time, the watching as each piece goes exactly as it must, exactly as it is planned to go, never outside the tolerances or the boundaries. Endless sameness forever and ever, world without end."

He laid a hand on the clock, and the turquoise lightning flowed to meet his hand from the other side.

"At last," he said and Marielle thought that she could almost hear singing from inside the clock as if it were calling to him.

274

A ray of dawn light hit the stained glass clock face, gleaming and filtering through to the burning dome behind it, warped by the heat of the flame.

"My suffering is over!" Etienne said and it was like a prayer. He turned to her, beaming with joy. "And yours has just begun."

# SPELLEND

# LAST DAY
## OF
# DAWNSPELL

# 33: GRANDFATHER TIMELESS

*TAMERLAN*

"Come on, come on!" Jhinn said, pulling the gondola up to the edge of the canal while Tamerlan lit his roll-up with a shaking hand from the flame in the lantern hanging from the ferro.

He shouldn't be doing this. It was going to be a disaster. He shouldn't be tempting fate by calling on forces he didn't understand, but these few fires were only the beginning. If he didn't find a way to get Abelmeyer's Eye from whatever Legend was controlling Etienne – likely Grandfather Timeless – then there wouldn't be any way to stop that dragon before it finished torching H'yi.

Besides, Etienne had Marielle. And Tamerlan was the one who had asked her to come with him here. He was responsible for her. He'd told her he would keep her safe, that all she needed to do was track the magic. And he hadn't protected her from being snatched from under his nose.

*Why are you doubting this now?* Lila asked. *You need us. You can't let the Fatemaker make your fate.*

Maybe he wasn't here to free his avatar. Maybe he'd gone somewhere else.

*You underestimate the power that the draw of freedom has over a man,* Deathless Pirate interjected. *Freedom is the greatest treasure.*

Okay, it was time to do this if he was going to, or he'd lose his chance to do anything about this mess. He needed to smoke now and hope he'd be taken by a friendly Legend and not a horrific one.

"Come on!" Jhinn called.

Please, not Maid Chaos. Please, not Maid Chaos.

With trembling hands, he brought the roll up to his lips as cries for bucket chains broke out around him.

"It's in the cathedral roof!"

"Dragon's spit!"

"Legends preserve us! Not the Cathedral of the Clock!"

They were dipping the buckets down on ropes into the canal, nearly smacking Jhinn's gondola as they threw them in without looking or thinking.

The first ray of dawn sparkled through the empty spaces between the temples and shrines around the canal as he drew in a long, lingering breath of smoke.

Please, not Maid Chaos.

Another puff. And then another, shuddering through his lungs as he hoped and prayed he wasn't making another disastrous mistake.

The ray of sun disappeared. The voices around him quieted.

Tamerlan looked up to see the light-colored belly-scales of a dragon skimming over them. His breath caught in his throat as the spire of the Cathedral of the Clock crunched and folded, raining to the ground in pieces as the dragon's belly skimmed the Temple District.

He didn't have time to breathe out before his consciousness was taken over by a familiar Legend.

*Hi, pretty man. Looks like it's us again.*

There was a strange sensation as if Tamerlan's insides were being pulled out through his nose and ears and then pain shot through him. Lila's voice was gone and another voice – this one deep and manly – filled his mind.

*What madness is this?*

He stumbled. What happened to Lila?

*She is not the hero for this time. Or this place. I sense one of the five dragons.*

Yes! And it was attacking H'yi!

*Disaster! We will stop this dragon.*

Tamerlan almost sagged with relief. He'd lucked into a Legend willing to help!

*It wasn't luck. I have taken the reins. This shouldn't be left to peasants and apprentices. The fate of the cities lies in your hands. The future of nations.*

Yes!

*We must find the Eye.*

It was with Grandfather Timeless.

His body froze.

*The Grandfather has Abelmeyer's Eye?*

Yes!

*My amulet has been taken by the Fatemaker? Dragon's blood in a pot! This is disaster!*

Could that really be King Abelmeyer in his mind? Tamerlan's mental eyes were wide with surprise as his body leapt off the gondola racing up the steps, dodging buckets and fire brigade chains. He ducked under a slopping pail. Clutching his sword scabbard to keep it from catching on anything.

They were rushing toward the cathedral. The roof was alight with flame. Long tendrils of orange flame like a blossoming flower licked down the sides of the cathedral as the fire spread. And there, in front of the building stood a massive clock. Wings formed the pediments and the tips of their feathers the finials. It glowed with power, the hands whirling around the face of the clock as if time had gone mad.

*It has gone mad! The Fatemaker is here! Many are the tales of the Grandfather, feared among fates, hated by mortals. He steals joy, crumbles*

280

*power, cripples even the strongest man, and steals the beauty of the fairest of maids. He is cruel and indiscriminate in his ravages across the earth.*

King Abelmeyer sped through the crowds, not bothering to stop or look when a blow from his shoulder accidentally sent one man spinning over the rail and into the canal.

*No time for that! There is a dragon in the sky and the Fatemaker stands before the clock that we built to keep him at bay!*

Wait. The clock was built for Grandfather Timeless?

*How else do you harness time? How else do you slice it up into tiny pieces and whittle down its power? You must contain it somehow. Analysis is the death of power. Close monitoring can bring down even the most energetic of foes.*

Interesting. Abelmeyer was drawing his sword – a dangerous thing to do in streets so full of bodies. His gaze was on the sky, watching as the head of the dragon spun around and flamed something in the distance – something that looked like the Palace in the center of the Government District.

*The Palace of the Nine Blossoms. A beautiful place. I drew up the plans for it myself.*

Was there anything he hadn't done?

*I was unable to find a way to bind the dragons permanently. Their binding must be renewed every year. In blood.*

Yeah. And that was a problem.

*All good things require sacrifice. And we always pay with our lives.*

But it wasn't him who was paying. It was innocent girls.

*It was our blood debt. It was our tithe – the promise of the Dragonblooded to defend the world from what we wrought.*

We?

They pushed past a woman hefting a yoke with two buckets dangling from chains and the moment they were past her, Tamerlan saw up the long steps to the foot of the Grandfather Clock.

Marielle! He'd found her!

Etienne held her by the hair, but she lunged forward, biting him. Way to go!

He ripped something from his neck. It glittered red in the sun.

"No!" Abelmeyer bellowed, racing forward, sword brandished high in the air. Tamerlan felt himself screaming with the King, his heart racing as the fires burned all around them in the streets and the smoke blurred their vision with puffs of acrid black.

By the time they reached the bottom of the stairs, Etienne had grabbed one of her hands, slicing it with his knife and pressing it to the base of the clock.

The lower door of the Clock of Ages opened with a rock-on-rock scraping squeal. It stood three stories high and as the door opened, the lightning around the pendulum sped up so that it arced up and down the pendulum at an alarming rate.

Time seemed to freeze and suddenly movement was painfully slow.

Abelmeyer fought it, his feet desperately trying to climb against the frozen air.

"Nooooot," he said, the word slowly squeezing from his lungs.

Etienne – unaffected by the frozen time – slung the chain suspending the Eye over Marielle's head as her eyes widened with horror.

"Thhhhhheeee," Abelmeyer said, leaping higher and freezing in the air as he tried to take the steps three at a time.

Etienne dragged Marielle to her feet. Her mouth was frozen in an "O" shape and her body seemed to drag against frozen time while Etienne's movements were easy and free. Something dropped from her hand, hanging frozen in the air. It glowed yellow for a moment.

"Eyyyyyyyeeee!" Abelmeyer finished, landing on the top step in slow motion.

Etienne's eyes flashed with delight at the sight of Tamerlan. With a cruel smile, he placed his hand on Marielle's frozen chest and pushed her into the clock.

Etienne froze the second she stumbled through the door. She was the one moving quickly now, her bindings falling off, her scream piercing the silence as she fell into the depths of the lightning-filled clock and the pendulum passed through her body. She flickered. Frozen. Turned white and translucent, frozen in screaming horror.

A translucent figure stepped out from the exact place she was standing. An old man, beard long, top hat and coat meticulously kept. As he strode past the door of the clock, he began to pick up color – pale at first and then darkening by hue so that by the time he reached Etienne, seizing him by the collar and dragging him from the door, he was almost fully opaque.

Full, bright color flashed into the old man's reddened face and rheumy eyes. The yellow thing Marielle had been holding dropped to the ground and Etienne stumbled forward and fell down the steps.

Time had returned.

A moment too late.

# 34: PENDULUM

Marielle couldn't move. She couldn't catch her breath. She felt her arms and legs frozen in place as she flickered in an out of the clock. When she was in the clock, she could see the world beyond it – the flames of the burning city. Tamerlan – face certain and noble – brandishing a huge sword as he lunged toward The Grandfather.

When she was not in the clock she was floating through space – not human at all – she was time personified. She made the grass grow and the seconds tick by. She watched the sun rise and fall and the moon wax and wane.

Human.

Not human.

Human.

Not human.

It was becoming hard to remember who she was at all.

285

Had it been seconds or hours or years?

Who could even know?

# 35: Abelmeyer's Eye

## TAMERLAN

King Abelmeyer swung his sword, a devastating overhand strike toward Grandfather Timeless. Tamerlan felt his mental teeth gritting against the blow. But the sword plunged through his ethereal body, sweeping out the other side and sending Tamerlan tottering forward, off balance.

"I'm not all the way here, yet!" Grandfather Time screeched. "You can't – "

Abelmeyer reached out, grabbing the Legend by his golden waistcoat and pulling him in close so he could speak right into his face.

"What comes out can go back in," he said, fist quivering with emotion. "That clock is your prison, and your term is not yet served."

The man cackled. "I broke the binding when I put a substitute in the clock. To put me back, you'd need to bind me again. And what will you bind me with? The Eye is on *her* neck!"

"If I take it off," Abelmeyer growled, "I can use it to bind you."

"And let that dragon go free?" the Grandfather's eyes twinkled. He found this amusing? Playing with the fates of innocents?

*Of course, he does. He's the villain in this story.*

How did Abelmeyer know?

*He's one of the villains in every story. Tell me, boy. What can steal your love and happiness? Only time and death.* He paused. *I can only bind one thing at a time with my Eye and if I use it to bind him again, the dragon will go free.*

"It was never in your nature to let cities burn," the Grandfather said, slipping out of Abelmeyer's hold and leaping away. Abelmeyer swiped for him, but he was too fast. He scrambled down the steps, leaping over Etienne as the Lord Mythos was still recovering, his head in his hands, blood flowing from bite marks down his arm.

With a roar of frustration, Abelmeyer spun, cutting Tamerlan's palm on the tip of his own sword and pressing his palm to the clock.

*You are Dragonblooded. I feel your blood pulsing in your veins. It sings to me.*

A horrifying thought.

*We offer your blood to keep the clock door open a few moments longer.*

Would that free her? Would it free Marielle?

*Nothing can free her now. She is the substitute. You can't trade her for another person, only for the true thing - the Grandfather.*

Then why hadn't the Grandfather kept the Eye? Why leave it here?

*He can't use it again. He doesn't have what it requires, so he leaves it here to delay us.*

Abelmeyer stepped inside the clock, sword still raised.

Marielle flickered into view and then flickered away again like the flame of a candle flickering – frozen in a horrified scream. Tamerlan's heart froze in his chest, his breath catching. He couldn't leave her like that. Not Marielle. She was the best of them all, the *most* worthy of life.

Not Marielle!

Abelmeyer snatched the Eye from around her neck and stepped back but Tamerlan reached out with his hand to stroke the side of her face and Abelmeyer let him. One flickering caress and then she was gone again. He felt a lurch in his chest.

He couldn't leave her like this.

Abelmeyer spun them around and leapt back out of the clock, letting the door close behind him. The door of the clock shut with the finality of a sepulchre.

No! They couldn't leave her! Tamlerlan shook himself mentally. It wasn't leaving Marielle – not forever. They had to get to the Grandfather and bind him with the Eye.

People were stumbling up the steps now as the fire in the Church of the Clock claimed more of the ancient building. The dome collapsed in a roar behind them as a priest stumbled forward, falling to his knees beside them, his eyes on the clock.

"He wasn't supposed to actually be real," he said, his voice hollow.

"Then why did you worship him?" Abelmeyer spat. Why was he wasting time? They needed to run through the crowd. They needed to chase the Grandfather!

*It's never the wrong time to set someone straight.*

Etienne was also on his feet, climbing the steps in a daze. Tamerlan recognized that lost look. He'd seen it in the mirror.

Etienne sounded numb as he spoke. "He was supposed to help me set time backward. We were going to restore Jingen. Return to a time before the dragon rose up."

Abelmeyer glanced up at the face of the clock. The hands had returned to normal, ticking the minutes and seconds at their normal speed.

"Things that happen, stay happened," he said grimly. "There are no second chances."

"We need to get her out of the clock," Etienne said, his voice catching. "I never meant ... I thought ..."

"No," Abelmeyer said quietly. "The Eye can only bind one thing at a time."

Tamerlan reached down and picked up the yellow thing she had been holding. A single shell. Abelmeyer let him have that much control. Let him put it in his pouch. Let him shed a single tear before he spoke again with Tamerlan's voice.

"The clock has her now. She can only come out if she is replaced by the Grandfather again."

"Then we chase him down," Etienne said grimly.

Of course they would. They would put him back in the clock!

Abelmeyer looked up to the sky where the dragon wheeled again. Around them, screams filled the air. The fires were spreading. Buildings were collapsing. Flames wreathed the city as the buckets of water were no longer enough.

Abelmeyer's voice roared through his mind. *You'd let the dragon burn these innocents to save one person? You'd trade all their lives for hers?*

Horror gripped Tamerlan's heart. That was the choice he made last time – though he didn't know it at the time. That was the burden he already bore. Marielle had said it was the wrong decision. She'd said he shouldn't have saved her. And he already had thousands of lives to atone for.

And yet – and yet he wanted to do it all again. He wanted to free her from the clock.

He wanted to, but he couldn't.

With a wrench that shook him to the core, he pulled his gaze away, looking to the sky where the dragon was just a silhouette across the sun. From this height at the Temple District, he saw it wheeling over the farm fields to the south-east where the Cerulean parted into the North and South branches.

Jingen had to be stopped. Whatever it took.

*Good boy. And now we will require a little more of your blood, hmm?*

"We will choose the dragon," he said aloud as if the declaration was needed.

Abelmeyer threw the chain over his neck, letting the Eye fall to his chest. This close, the flaw in the stone did look like an eye winking at him.

*It was my eye before I gave it up for this purpose.*

The thought of that made Tamerlan's stomach heave.

*Sacrifice. To use it, a similar sacrifice will be required of you.*

Wait.

No.

No, no, no!

Realization of what King Abelmeyer meant filled him immediately.

*If you want to use the eye, you have to give an eye.*

No!

Panic shot up through him like icy daggers, sinking into his spine, his heart, his brain.

*Does this mean you have changed your mind?*

He shook himself. He had so much to redeem himself for. No sacrifice was too great … was it?

"I'll do it." He'd been allowed his own voice to say those words, though it quavered with fear even as he said them.

Would the King gouge it out right here and now? Would he do it with the sword? Plunge it into Tamelerlan's eye and –?

His thoughts cut off as the vision from one of his eyes winked out, like a blown out candle. He gasped.

*It's magic. You won't have to lose the physical eye. Not like I did.*

Half of his sight was gone.

And just like that, the far-away dragon dropped from the sky.

Around him, the breath in a thousand throats caught as the people of the city watched the dragon fall in the golden light of morning. He hit the earth so hard that the city shook beneath their feet, the half-burned buildings around them collapsing with a *boom*.

Earth and vegetation shot up into the air around the fallen dragon and Tamerlan felt an ache in his chest as he saw the dragon fall.

It had worked.

H'yi was saved – mostly.

There would still be fires to put out. Still rebuilding to accomplish. But most of the city still stood, and the dragon did not. How long would he sleep?

*With what I've done? As long as he is bound by the Eye. Keep it close.*

He tucked it into his shirt, carefully hiding it from sight.

As his hand left the chain, he felt the Legend fade from his mind.

With a choked cry, Tamerlan slumped against the clock, his forehead against the glass. He'd made the right choice, hadn't he? *This time* he'd made the right choice.

Then why did it feel like the wrong one? Why did it feel like he'd sold Marielle's soul and his along with it?

The vision of his single eye was making him dizzy. He closed it, gritting his teeth and hammering at the door, but all the blood of his hands did not open the door. Not even when he beat against it until every knuckle was a bloody pulp and the tracks of his blood ran down the front of the clock like spatters of rain.

Maybe it needed Grandfather Timeless there, too. But now he had nothing to bind the Legend with and no way to free Marielle.

Tears tracked down his face as he screamed her name, battering the door of the clock with his fists.

# EPILOGUE

*TAMERLAN*

"Tamerlan," a gentle voice said eventually, pulling him away from the clock. "I don't think you can get in that way."

The Lord Mythos sounded tired as he pulled Tamerlan away and helped him sit on the edge of the stairs.

"You chose the dragon," he said and there was no emotion in his dead voice as he said. "I would have done the same thing."

Tamerlan choked down a sob. He wanted to smoke again and let a Legend take him, but there was never a happy ending when they did.

"I don't have bandages here," Etienne said after a while. They were both still bleeding – Tamerlan from the wound on his hand. Etienne from the bites on his arm. "Let's find you somewhere safe. Did the boy with the gondola come with you?"

"Yes," Tamerlan said weakly, turning his head to look at the clock. Everything looked strange through just one eye.

"Come on. Let's find him."

Tamerlan sheathed his sword – it took two tries – and then Etienne led him down the steps and through the crowd.

The people had gathered in the streets and anyone not desperately fighting the fires stared into the distance where the dragon had fallen as if they still couldn't believe it.

As they walked down the steps, the sky opened, and rain began to fall – torrents of it. It washed over the Clock of Ages. It poured in sheets over the fires. It soaked every soul to the bone in seconds, running in black rivulets of ash and soot down the streets and over the edges into the canals.

On Spellend, the day when all were washed clean, the water poured over H'yi, washing away the fury of the dragon, the blood of the Dragonblooded on the Clock of Ages, and the fear they'd all felt as the dragon destroyed H'yi. It washed over the devastation and frantic searchers in Xin. It poured over the tumbled ruins of Jingen. It flowed out down the rivers and into the sea, rippling out to the waiting ships of The Retribution. It soaked the fallen dragon in the crater he'd made in the earth.

No drop of salvation touched Marielle in her clock. No cleansing flood covered her.

And wet though he was on the outside, Tamerlan knew that the forgiveness of the heavens was not for him. He knew that he could never be washed clean. Not until the Legend was back in the clock. Not until the woman he cared about was free again. Not until he'd paid more than just the sight of one eye to save them all.

\*\*\*

I hope that you enjoyed reading Dawnspell as much as I enjoyed writing it. You can continue with the story in *Autumngale: Book Three of the Bridge of Legends* or chat with us about it in the Discord group.

# BEHIND THE SCENES:

USA Today bestselling author, Sarah K. L. Wilson loves spinning a yarn and if it paints a magical new world, twists something old into something reborn, or makes your heart pound with excitement ... all the better! Sarah hails from the rocky Canadian Shield in Northern Ontario - learning patience and tenacity from the long months of icy cold - where she lives with her husband and two small boys. You might find her building fires in her woodstove and wishing she had a dragon handy to light them for her

Sarah would like to thank **Harold Trammel** and **Eugenia Kollia** for their incredible work in beta reading and proofreading this book. Without their big hearts and passion for stories, this book would not be the same.

Sarah has the deepest regard for the talent of her phenomenal artists – **Francesca Baerald** who designed the gorgeous map for this series and Lius Lasahido and his team at **Polar Engine** who created the gorgeous cover art that accompanies this book. Without their work, it would be so much harder to show off this story the way it deserves!

*www.sarahklwilson.com*